Dayr
melt that ice,
baby!

HAT
TRICK

SPORTS ROMANCE

BY:
KRISTEN HOPE
MAZZOLA

HAT TRICK
Copyright © 2016 Kristen Hope Mazzola
Published by Kristen Hope Mazzola

Published: Kristen Hope Mazzola 2016

Cover Design: Kristen Hope Mazzola
Cover Images:
Model: Lance Jones - Tattoo model
Photographer: Kruse Images & Photography: Models & Boudoir
Formatting by: Kristen Hope Mazzola

Editing by:
C. Marie: editingbycmarie@gmail.com

Proof Reading by:
Patti Correa: shore2pleaseedits@gmail.com

DEDICATION:

To anyone that has been kicked in the balls by love and still believes in it, this one is for you.

PROLOGUE

Myla

Deep slow breaths.

I could feel every muscle in my body getting ready.

See the jump.

Know how it is going to go.

Feel every movement.

Visualize.

One...

Two...

Three...

I could fly. In those few seconds, I could actually fly.

Pushing myself to limits I never thought possible was incredibly liberating, and pulling off the perfect flying camel was always my favorite. There was something so peaceful about being alone in the rink. My skates gliding over slick, smooth, polished ice...the chilly air nipping at my cheeks and filling my lungs...it was like coming home.

I knew I was meant to be there.

Skating around, listening to my Spotify playlist full of angsty punk rock music—it was the best way to fill an afternoon. Right as Blink-182 started singing about going away to college, my skates left the ice and I was in complete bliss.

After landing my best inside axel ever, my eyes snapped to the bleachers to find my mother's smiling face. She was absolutely radiant, practically glowing as she jumped to her feet, clapping and cheering.

"Do a stag for me!" She beamed as she cupped her hands around her mouth to project her voice out to reach me.

I rolled my eyes, yelling back to her, "Why do you like splits so much? I just don't get it."

She giggled, shrugging. "What can I say? I just do."

"As you wish," I teased, sticking my tongue out at her as I skated backward to get enough room to pull off her request.

I set myself up, taking a few slow, deep breaths, counting to myself. Within seconds I was flying again, smiling at my mother as she collapsed where she stood up in the stands. I crashed down onto the ice as a blaring horn drowned out my music.

My eyes burst open. Lights were all I could see— bright lights barreling toward us. I was strapped into the passenger's seat. The windshield wipers were frantically trying to keep up with the pouring, freezing rain.

I screamed as I realized what was actually happening. "Oh my God, Mom! A truck!"

Crash.

Darkness.

Stillness.

Nothing.

ONE

Brayden

"So, doc..." My eyes traveled down to the blue-gray speckled white floor of my sister's hospital room as I gripped her hand tighter. "How bad is it, really?" I knew from how mangled the car was that I was lucky she was breathing—even if it was with the help of a machine—but I needed to find a shred of hope that she'd see morning.

Watching Myla's tiny frame clinging to life in that hospital bed damn near broke me. Most of the time, I prided myself on being the tough one in the family, but right then and there I was crumbling into a pile of useless emotions, praying for this to all be one sick, twisted nightmare that I needed to wake from.

The young doctor with a thick red beard put his hand on my shoulder, frowning. "We're going to do everything we can to save her, Mr. Cox. Go home and get some sleep. We will know more in the morning."

I nodded, willing my eyes to travel up my sister's

bedside. The site of a breathing tube coming out of her mouth and the beeping of the machine that was acting as her lungs made my stomach lurch. The cuts and scratches that dappled her fair skin didn't do the severity of the crash justice. Both of her eyes were black and blue, her cheeks were swollen, and too many bones in her body were shattered. It was purely a miracle that the first responders were able to get her out of the car, let alone stabilize her enough to get her to the hospital and into surgery in time, but they managed it somehow.

I squeezed her hand one last time, bending down and whispering into her ear, "Myla, if you can hear me, please fight. Please be strong. You're all I got left. I love you, sis." I cursed the tear that rolled down my cheek onto hers as I kissed my little sister's temple.

Squeaking sneakers sounded behind me. Turning slowly, I locked eyes with a short nurse in purple scrubs sheepishly walking into the room. Her petite figure reminded me of Myla's, and she had a tiny bounce in her step that made her short, stick-straight hair sway side to side with every step. "Sorry, I just need to check on her." She bit her bottom lip, looking down at Myla's chart near the foot of her bed.

Taking a few steps back to let the nurse do her job, I cleared my throat. "Is it okay if I stay the night here with her?"

The nurse frowned with her entire tiny frame

while shaking her head. "I'm afraid that's not allowed in critical care, sir. Visiting hours start at seven and end at nine."

I glanced down at my watch to see that I was already overstaying my welcome by an hour. Failing at forming a smile, I shoved my hands into my pockets. "All right. I'll be on my way."

Her kind eyes searched mine as more damned tears welled up and a lump the size of Long Island formed in my throat. "I'm Karla. I'm working all night." She reached into her pocket and pulled out a business card and a pen. "Write your cell number here. I'll call you personally if anything happens."

With shaking hands, I did as she asked with more gratitude than I had thought possible. "I don't really know how to thank you for this." My voice was weak and fading.

As I handed her back the business card, I realized how wobbly my hands were. The nerves and worry were starting to get the better of me.

"Just try to get some rest. Here." She handed me another business card. "Just in case you get worried during the night, my cell number is on there."

"I appreciate it."

In what seemed like the blink of an eye, I was making my way to the parking garage on autopilot. Everything was turning into a blur. Unlocking my car, putting my seatbelt on, putting the car in drive—it all felt like I was watching a movie, not actually experiencing it myself. Pulling into the garage at my parents' house shocked my senses awake; I didn't even remember pulling onto Elm Street or rounding the corner onto Addison.

Throwing my keys onto my dresser, I fell back onto my king-sized bed. I didn't know how I was still moving, breathing, thinking—I just knew I had to keep it up. Myla had to be all right and I had to be strong for her. In just one phone call, my entire life had flipped over on top of me, crushing every bit of my soul. All at once, it hit me—my anger, my rage, my temper. Within minutes, my meticulously manicured room rumbled into a mirror of the torment of my situation.

After I released all the tension, a wave of realization flooded me. As I stood in the middle of my oversized room with the glass from my mirror scattered around the floor, blood coming from my busted knuckles, and a few new holes that needed to be patched peppering my walls, I couldn't escape the reality of the day's occurrences any longer.

My mother was dead and my sister was in a medically induced coma because of her extensive injuries. The guilt was overwhelming. There was nothing I could have done to prevent the truck from running that stoplight or make my mother buckle her seatbelt, but I was the man of the house and the responsibility of protecting my family was mine to bear.

The hours ticked by until exhaustion took over. I was startled awake by my alarm clock chiming loudly in my ear, and I realized I was still wearing my sweats and long-sleeved shirt from the practice I had been ripped away from when the hospital called.

Checking my phone, I saw a few texts from teammates checking up on me, a few voicemails from my assistant coach, and a text from an unsaved number.

Swiping open my phone, I read words that brought tears of relief to my eyes:

> **Just letting you know, your sister did great overnight. I gave your number to the day nurse and will check in later to see how you two are doing. Take care – Karla.**

I quickly rattled off a reply:

> **Thank you for letting me know. I am heading that way now. Hope you get some rest after a long night shift.**

After a quick shower, a few bites of cold pizza from a few nights back, and a call to my coach, I made the drive back to the hospital.

Just be strong.

Breathe.

Deep...slow...breaths.

Everything is going to be fine.

She's going to be fine.

Myla

Pain and confusion completely consumed every cell in my body.

"Myla?" Brayden's voice sounded miles away. "Myla? Can you hear me?"

I tried to respond but nothing would come out. My throat was a desert begging to rain out words that formed questions and cries for help.

My hair was being stroked, but my eyes refused to open to see who was caring for me. I pictured my mother's dainty hand gliding over my thin blonde locks as my brother tried to speak to me.

Where am I?

Why does everything hurt?

Why can't I speak?

Why aren't my eyes opening?

A foreign voice that was barely audible started to explain something to my brother. "...and that's why she's still really out of it. She will be in and out like this for a little bit longer. Why don't we let her sleep some more and try back in a few hours?"

Sleep sounded all too blissful. I felt like Scarlett O'Hara in the scene where she is at Tara and life is just all too much for her to deal with in that moment. *"I can't think about that right now. If I do, I'll go crazy. I'll think about that tomorrow."*

Soft beeping broke into my dream-filled daze as my eyelids struggled to open. Shuffling and footsteps were the next sounds I could understand.

"Mom?" My voice was raspy and strained as tears started to fill my stinging eyes.

My brother's deep voice was kind. "No, My. It's just me." I could feel his fingertips brushing my long bangs away from my forehead and cheeks. "It's nice to see you awake."

"What?" I started choking, gasping, and coughing uncontrollably. Everything hurt—my throat, chest, legs, stomach, back, face, eyes, lips. I was shivering and sweating. My body felt like it weighed a million pounds. If my hair could have hurt, I was sure it would have been screaming in pain at that point.

"You were in an accident. Do you remember anything?" Brayden's calm tone was freaking me out the most.

The memories of the crash started to flood my mind and I started hyperventilating. "Mom? Where's

Mom?"

Brayden's fingers laced with mine as he started to tell me about the accident. "I'm so sorry, Myla. I don't know how to tell you this."

My eyes would barely open and the tears filling them made it damn near impossible to see, but the pain on my brother's face was something I would never be able to forget. That moment was seared into my brain—the split second when life turned into a complete horror.

Two

Gavin

Grabbing a handful of bar peanuts, I shoveled them into my mouth. "This joint really needs to start making some damn food or something. I'm starving." I chucked a peanut right at Sean's ear, missing.

Damn it. At least I have better aim on the ice.

My best friend rolled his eyes at me. "One week left of singlehood. Man, are you ready?" Sean chuckled a little before taking another gulp from his three-fingers pour of Jameson.

I shrugged. "As ready as I'll ever fucking be. I'm just ready to get this whole thing over with."

Sean slapped my shoulder harder than most would find friendly, but that was just how we were with each other. "It's going to be great man. I'm really excited for you and Marsheila."

"You fucking hate her. You're not fooling anyone." I rolled a maraschino cherry around in my mouth, savoring the sweetness for a second.

He gasped dramatically, putting his hand to his chest. "When have I ever said anything of the sort?"

"Come on, dude, you know I'm right. How about every fucking time you've been drunk since the day I told you I was going to ask Marsheila to marry me? It's been nonstop slurs of 'You're making a huge mistake, man. Don't do it, dude. That old ball and chain is going to ruin your fucking life.'"

"Me? No, I would never." Sean flashed a quick grin. "What kind of best friend would I be if I didn't question the biggest decision of your life?"

I shrugged. "A crappy one, I guess, but still, we're a week away. I think we both know this is going to happen."

Sean threw up his hands. "You're right. I was only looking out for your best interest. If that's marrying the Wicked Witch of the West, then by all means, be my guest."

"You barely even know her." I slammed my empty glass down in front of the bartender. "Bar temptress, another."

She pushed her short black pixy-style hair away from her face with the back of her hand, giving me the stink eye. "You know I cannot stand it when you call me that, Gavin."

She started to make my second Manhattan, giving me a coy smile. "Oh come on, Jordan, you know I'm just messing with you."

Jordan smiled at me, setting the glass down on the soaked coaster then putting two cherries in, just the way I liked. "You haven't changed one bit since high school. You're still the same pompous jerkoff you've always been."

I took a long swig. "Yes, and that's why you love me."

She grabbed her stomach as she let out a deep laugh, slapping her tiny hand onto the counter. "In your fucking dreams, Gavin. In your fucking dreams."

Jordan would never admit it, but Sean and I were the only two people she even remotely tolerated from our graduating class. The three of us had been a little wolf pack since any of us could remember, growing up just a few houses apart in the old neighborhood near Huntington Station.

It helped that we were some of the few that went different routes than the conventional college education after high school. Jordan Bates was one of the best bartenders in the city; she even went around the country helping bars train their new drink slingers. Sean was one of New York City's finest; wearing that blue uniform suited him well and he burst with pride every time we talked about it. And me, I was the hooligan of the bunch, playing hockey for the New York Otters.

Even though hockey was my dream, it was a hard

sell. Most people thought I had lucked into the role because of my old man. It didn't help that I was drafted to the team he fucking coached—that fact actually made my life a living hell. Of course, I was proud to wear the red, white, and blue uniform—I had wanted to since I was a little kid, but that had been back when my dad was still my hero, not a washed-up jackass that treated me like the scum of the earth.

"Sean, how was work today?" Jordan started cleaning up the bar, our cue that it was getting close to time to get the heck out of Dodge.

Sean slouched back in his seat. "It was a fucking day of it to say the least."

Usually, Sean was pretty forthcoming with stories from his day. He loved telling us about all the crazy shit people tried to pull, lies they thought would get them out of whatever charges were about to be brought against them, how stupid some people could really be, etc. When he kept quiet, we knew something seriously messed up had happened during his shift. Jordan poured him a few more fingers of whiskey as his eyes started to well up with tears. We both knew that meant they had lost someone that day, and we sure as shit weren't going to press the issue. If Sean wanted to talk about it, he would.

He stared down at the amber liquid, his pointer finger tracing the rim of the glass. "It's sad when a parent dies but their kid survives. It's miserable when anyone dies, but a mother dying in front of her daughter in a car crash is downright awful." He slammed back the rest of his drink and grabbed his coat from the stool next to him. "I think it's time to call it a night. See you guys at the rehearsal dinner?"

"Yeah, man. See you Friday."

Shaking hands—check.

Sweat dripping down my ass crack—check.

Everyone's eyes glaring at me while I stand outside in the blaring sun with a goddamned bowtie nearly choking me to death—check.

I couldn't believe two years had flown by the way it had. Ms. Marsheila Rhodes was about to be Mrs. Marsheila Hayes and my life was going to fall into place perfectly like I had always thought it was going to. We even had an offer in on a little house out in the 'burbs with a large front porch and a damn white picket fence.

How sappy can I get?

I wasn't usually such a fucking-sentimental-ass-goober, but standing under a pink and white flower-covered altar with the chick officiant giving me a reassuring *Don't worry honey, this will all be over before you know it* smile and my best friend patting my shoulder with a *This is going to be an awesome day, bud* gleam in his eye...it was starting to get to me.

We waited...and we waited...and we freaking waited some more.

Fuck, where is this woman?

The music from the string quartet was starting to get on my nerves as they started to play their set for a third time. Our guests were fidgeting in their white folding chairs as they looked around, muttering to themselves. It was starting to get pretty embarrassing.

"What the heck is taking them so damn long?" I mumbled to Sean, wiping the beading sweat off my forehead.

He just shrugged, shaking his head. "You know how Marsheila has to be perfect. They're probably still trying to get her hair just right."

This waiting game was getting absolutely ridiculous. We were already running thirty minutes late. At the current rate, we were going to miss our cocktail hour completely, which was the only part of the whole event I actually was looking forward to. The rest of the day I had agreed to just to make the little wifey smile.

Happy wife, happy life.

Happy wife, happy life.

Happy wife, happy life.

I had to keep reminding myself why I had thrown

so much money down the drain for one fucking party. Seventy grand flushed down the toilet for five hours of mingling with people, half of whom I couldn't stand or didn't even know.

What a fucking crock of shit.

Out of the corner of my eye I saw Hillary, my soon-to-be-wife's little sister, start quickly shuffling around the group of seated guests, trying to wave me over to her.

Hillary's eyes were glassy and wide as her hands trembled, handing me a note. I stared at her, shaking my head. A tear rolled down her face as she whispered, "I am so sorry, Gavin. I couldn't talk her out of it." She shoved the note into my hand before turning around and bolting away in her tan heels and short flowing seafoam dress.

I dropped to my knees right there in the soft damp grass.

I didn't want to know why—all I needed to know was that my life had shifted on its axis in one second flat.

Sean started to pull me up by my armpits, forcing me to stand. I couldn't control it—I was fucking raging, slipping into shock, and I took it out on the closest target. I clocked my best friend right in the jaw. Tears were streaming down my face as he grabbed his cheek, staggering backward a bit. "Holy fuck man!"

I was frozen. All eyes were on me. No one was moving, not a word was spoken. My heart was crumbling. The silence was maddening.

Sean wrapped me up in hug, wrestling the note out of my hands.

"Get off of me!" I was seeing red as I screamed into his face.

"You just punched me, dude. You need to let me see this." His eyes were locked on mine as I thought about pulling his shirt over his head like a jersey, but my better judgment kicked in just in time. I gave in and watched as Sean opened the handwritten note from my now ex-fiancée. His eyes got wider and wider as they read down the page.

"Fuck her man. Let's go get fucking drunk."

I tried to take the note from his hands. "Why don't you just wait until tomorrow for this? Let's make the best of all the money you blew on this shit show."

Sean put the note in his pocket and I turned to the guests. "It seems like there won't be a wedding tonight, I guess that's something to celebrate."

So, in our tuxes, with all the guests that were there for me, we went and got plastered at the open bar, ate a shit load of amazing filet mignon with wild Alaskan salmon along with everything else at the buffet, and danced our night away. The best part by far was the food fight the ensued once the cake was brought out. The extra cleaning and damages bill that came a few days later was totally worth it.

I had paid for that shit; I figured I might as well use

it to begin the next chapter of my life as a fucking single man. The evening turned out to not be what was expected, but it was one of the best nights in my life—a complete and total liberation of Gavin Hayes.

THREE

Brayden

"Way to fuck up out there today, rookie. At this rate, you're going to make a great duster." Gavin snickered as we walked past each other in the locker room.

"Thanks." I rolled my eyes. There wasn't much to say, which fucking sucked. I hated biting my tongue.

He smelled like absolute dick as he dripped with sweat, walking over to the showers. His cocky ass smirk made me want to deck him right there, but punching the coach's son was probably not going to be a good move when I had just joined the team. Hazing was expected; all the guys gave me a hard time and I had tough skin, but there was just something about Gavin that I couldn't fucking stand. It probably went back to the days when our dads were teammates. Our rivalry very well could have been our own, but it likely bled from our fathers' propaganda.

My dad was Reggie Cox, one of the best left wings the New York Otters had ever seen. He was named captain his second season and had that C on his chest until he was forced to retire due to a knee injury he sustained from being hooked in the middle of a playoff game. The Otters ended up losing the game and hadn't gone to the Stanley Cup since. That's when everything went to shit for my family. It was the beginning of my father's end, when he turned to the bottle and opiates, becoming the meanest son of a bitch on the fucking planet.

"Reg. Stop. You're hurting him." My mom pleaded as my father's grip tightened around my upper arm. I just glared at him for a few seconds; this was nothing new. I knew standing up to him would only make matters worse, but it was getting to the point where I just didn't care anymore.

"Dad, I promise I can do better." I tried to pull away, but that only made his nails turn in, digging slowly into my tender flesh, even through the jersey. Dad's power was a real bitch and he abused it knowingly.

"You're going to learn how to do this slap shot if we have to be here all night." His face was boiling red as he spit the words out at me, our noses barely an inch apart.

The rest of the team watched from the bench, most

of their jaws dropping to their chests as our coach reamed out their teammate again.

My mom leaned over the wall, trying to reach out to her husband—yet another failed attempt to break through his rage.

"Dad, please. I promise I will get it right this time."

"You fucking better, or you're going to be a damn good duster and Connor will be my new starting left forward. How would you like that?"

"I want to play." His grip finally loosened and I was able to skate back over to the rest of my teammates.

"Gentlemen, settle down." Coach Hayes cleared his throat for the hundredth time, adjusting his tie, fidgeting, and sweating.

"What's going on with Coach? He looks like he's about to start shitting bricks." Donaldson leaned over, muttering low enough that only I could hear him.

I shook my head, sitting in the rumbling locker room, hair still dripping from my post-practice shower. "I don't know, man."

Gavin Hayes stood up and went over to his father. "Shut the fuck up, guys. This is serious."

"Coach's son to the fucking rescue."

Donaldson was really starting to get on my nerves. Just because I was a rookie didn't mean I was someone he could bitch and moan to about the team. To me, we were all brothers—end of fucking story. Him acting like a teenage mean girl was going to eventually get him knocked the fuck out.

Ignore him. I had to keep reminding myself of the advice Myla force-fed me every night over dinner when I would come home and unleash all my pent up rage from the day.

"Men, we have to name a new captain. You all know Nikolaev isn't returning this season. Since my son is on the team, I have decided it's unfair for me to appoint our next one. Instead, we're going to put it to a vote. Everyone is eligible. Think of leadership. Who do you want to be your voice on the ice? Who do you trust enough to let them wear that C on their chest? Write his name down and put it in the locked box I have on my desk. This is the only fair way to do it."

We all took slips of paper and a bunch of the guys started chatting in the corner. It wasn't unheard of for a team to put selecting a new captain to a vote. It was respectable that Coach wanted to remain unbiased, particularly because it was clear that his son Gavin was the right man for the job. Personally, I thought he was a fucktard, but most of the guys respected the shit out of him and he was damn good at pep talks on the ice.

Staring at the blank piece of paper, I tried to come up with anyone else's name to write down. Nothing. Gavin was the going to be our next captain. He was going to make my life hell, but maybe I would become a better player because of it.

Gavin

"Cheers, to Gavin being named captain of the Otters. Who would have thought a fuck-up like you would ever become a leader of the team?"

I rolled my eyes, clanking my goblet against my brother's, my mother's, and finally my father's crystal glasses. "Thanks, Pop."

I cut into my rare steak, watching the juices pool on my mother's fine china—the crap she only brought out for special occasions. It meant a lot that she thought of this as a celebration, but who the fuck were we kidding? The team had only picked me because there was no better option, and the fact that Gideon Hayes was my father; they probably all thought that was what they were supposed to do.

Griffin gave me a quick eye roll followed by his reassuring wink, trying his best to laugh off my father's rude display of persistent disappointment in me. "Dad, don't be so hard on Gavin. He's the right man for the job— his teammates think so at least. It's good they trust him."

"Bunch of idiots if you ask me, but the majority had its say." Dad slurped his cabernet like a heathen, wiping the driblets from his brassily chin with the back of his hand. You can take the hick out of the backwoods and move him up to New York, dress him up in his Sunday best, but you can never take the backwoods out of the hick when booze and disappointment start to soak his blood.

"Gideon, you're drunk. Don't be mean." Mom always tried to just chalk the nasty shit Dad said up to being drunk. Usually, she was right, but I knew the crap currently spilling out of his wine-soaked mouth was his true feelings.

I knew the moment I was drafted to The Otters that my father was not going to be happy about it. He wanted me to go to any other team—then he could just be proud of his son and I would be some other coach's problem.

"Griffin, don't you have a fight coming up?" Anything to get the conversation away from me.

Griff sucked on his teeth while he nodded. "Yeah, I got challenged by Chuck Williams. I'm going to have to go up a weight class to meet him, but I'll never back down from a fight."

Griffin was my little brother by five years. He was fresh out of college and already making a huge name for himself as an up-and-coming boxer. *Sports News* had named him 'Fighter to Watch' this year, and I knew my dad was way more excited about that than anything I had done since the fifth grade.

"Griff is going to make this family proud, that's for damn sure."

Way to rub salt in the wound, Pop.

"How about that lovely girl, what was her name, Griffin? With the long dark hair?"

I started to laugh. "Which one?" I teased, and Griffin kicked me under the table.

"Things aren't really working out. I have been pretty busy training, too much to have time for a high-maintenance chick like Marissa."

"Marissa, that was it. She was lovely. You should still try, son. You don't find nice girls with such good breeding every day."

Breeding. My mother was all about the status of our relationships—if we were living up to our legacy with the women who were sucking us off at night. *Who the fuck cares?*

"We'll see what happens, Ma."

My little brother was the stereotypical New Yorker: thick accent, sharp dresser, knew everybody. The only things we had in common other than our last names and hatred for our old man were our love for ink and slutty women. Even though we were so different, I would do anything for the kid and he always had my back, too. It was a family thing. No one was going to mess with either of us if the other one had anything to say about it.

"What about you, Gavin?"

I looked up from my plate, steak rolling around in my mouth.

"Huh?" I knew it wasn't polite to talk with my mouth full, but after my father's display of his complete lack of table manners, I couldn't have cared less.

My mother sighed, glaring at me. She hated when I didn't act like the son she had raised. "Is there anyone special in your life? Do you have a lady-friend?"

I couldn't hold back my laughter. I nearly spit out my food before I had the chance to swallow it. "I think I am off women for the time being."

"Son, you're going to have to get back on the horse eventually. No one wants a weak captain that can't get laid because he's crying in the corner over some bitch leaving him at the altar."

Dad for the win.

"Well, I guess we're done here." I shoved away from the table, trying to cool my temper before I knocked my old man's teeth in.

"You sit your ass in your chair and respect your father."

I bowed my head, working my jaw as I took my seat. "Yes ma'am."

FOUR

Brayden

One Year Later

"Come back to bed." A soft moan came from my blue satin-covered king bed.

If I could only remember her damn name.

I rinsed out the toothpaste and spit into the sink, wiping away the white foam from the creases around my mouth with a hand towel before throwing it onto the marble sink. The old mahogany whined under my bare feet as I made my way back over to her.

Long bleached-blonde hair curled and frizzed around her face as she peacefully lay curled up in the groggy moments of leisurely waking up. The heavy makeup she had on from the night before was smudged around her eyes and running down her cheeks, probably from gagging on my cock only a few hours before. I loved when a girl really deep throated and tears streamed down her cheeks. There was something so raw and real about those encounters.

Damn blackouts. I wish I could remember more of our sexcapade.

The end of the night was a blur, unfortunately. She had caught my eye with her tighter than tight light blue dress, insanely high, very flattering heels, and bright pink lipstick. Add in how juicy her butt looked as she waggled by and I was a goner. It was right about the time the lights came on and the DJ started to play Journey's "Don't Stop Believin'". Before I knew it, we were making out in the backseat of a yellow cab, heading to my place. I did remember making her take her heels off as we snuck through the house—waking Myla up was very low on my to-do list, to say the least. My little sister did not need to hear me sneaking in another random fuck in the middle of the night.

I sat on the edge of the bed, sighing.

Too bad there isn't time for one more quickie.

"I have a lot to do today." *Hopefully she can take a subtle hint.*

I heard Myla's shower start.

"Damn it," I muttered under my breath.

"What is it, babe?" She sat up, running her dainty fingertips over my shoulder.

I tensed under her touch. "You really need to go. I'll get you a cab."

"Do you even know my name?" My dead eyes

darted to hers as I shook my head. "You fucking bastard."

I got up to hand her the blue dress I had thrown across the room. "I've been called worse."

I could see the blood boiling under her skin as she thought of all the foul things she wanted to call me. As the pissed-off chick started to pull her heels on, I saw the light bulb go off in her brain. Within seconds she was out of her leopard print pumps and throwing one directly at my head.

"Bitch. Get the fuck out of my house!" I yelled as the heel crashed onto my armoire behind me.

She stood there in the middle of my room, pouting, and her blaring green eyes would have killed me if that were possible.

"Make me." She popped out her hip and started tapping her bare feet on the area rug that surrounded my bed.

"Wrong answer." Right as I was about to pick her up and throw her over my shoulder to physically remove her from my home, Myla's small frame came into view in my doorway.

"Bray? What in God's name are you doing?"

The random girl gasped. "Who that fuck is this bitch?"

Wrong move. Myla was the epitome of the Shakespeare quote: *"Though she be but little, she is fierce."*

I grabbed Myla's wrist before she got close enough to slap the chick that was clearly from Staten Island—her style, accent, and entitlement issues gave it away in seconds.

"This is my sister, Myla, and again, it's time for you to go."

"Fine, whatever. You ain't worth my time anyway. Fucking hockey player. Oh well, everyone slums it for one night."

I rolled my eyes. Did she really think her words meant anything to me?

"All right cunt bag, there's the door. You know how to use one of those right?" Myla cracked me up. She was so sweet and innocent for the most part, but once her patience was tested, there was no saving you.

Myla

After yet another one-night stand huffed out of our house, I was easily able to bribe Brayden to make me breakfast. Usually, all it took was a puppy-dog face and a *please*, but this leverage was going to be fun to exploit. I was going to keep it in my back pocket for when I really needed it, but at the moment we had bigger fish to fry.

"I really don't think it's going to work out, Brayden." My big brother set a plate of scrambled egg whites with goat cheese, diced tomatoes, and spinach in front of me while I slurped my iced green tea. Then he took his seat across the table with the same meal in front of him. He knew the way to talk me into anything: my favorite foods.

With his bright amber eyes, Brayden beamed at me with all the encouragement a big brother could give to his kid sister. "Look, Myla, you have to do this. I am not going to sit by and let you waste away in this house. You need to get out there and do something!"

"Yeah, like you did last night?" It was a snarky jab, but I needed to stack the deck a little bit in my favor.

He rolled his eyes. "You know what I am talking about."

I pushed the eggs around my plate, whining. "But being a figure skating coach's assistant seems like a big fucking joke, Bray! I mean come on!" I was a little annoyed with Brayden for getting me the interview completely behind my back. It was nice of him, and sure, his heart was in the right place, but forcing me to get back on skates just a little more than a year after my hip and femur were fractured in the accident was a little more than I could wrap my head around.

"Mom would have wanted you to get back out there and you know it."

There it was, the line I hated, and he knew it. It crawled right under my skin and festered there. It broke my heart because he was right, and I hated the power that lay in his hands because of it.

"Look, Myla, I have to go back on the road in a week, and I want to know that you're going to be taking care of yourself. Doing this will be good for you. You need to meet people and get your nose out of those books for a little while, and with your physical therapy completed—"

"All right." I sighed, cutting my brother off with a harsh glance before shoving a huge bite into my mouth. I quickly heaved away from the table, leaving most of my breakfast on the plate. "I guess I better get ready and get my skates sharpened before I meet the head coach. What's his name anyway?"

Brayden's smile was infectious as he tried to hide how giddy he was that I had given in so easily. "It's Simon Abramson."

The name clicked and my mouth fell open. "The Simon Abramson? Like five-time gold medalist?"

Brayden nodded. "Yup, the one and only."

"How'd you...?" I was standing in the middle of our kitchen in complete shock.

"He comes in from time to time to help the team with some skating techniques. I got his number when he was bitching about losing his other assistant to maternity leave."

I shuffled my fuzzy pink slippers over to my big brother, threw my arms around his neck, and kissed him on the stubbly jawline. "Thanks." I smiled down at him. Even though it was going to be hard and I still didn't know how I'd feel once I was back out on the ice, it meant a lot to me that Brayden cared so much.

FIVE

Myla

After going through ten outfits, running down to the pro shop to get my old skates sharpened, and rushing like a maniac to get to the rink on time, I realized how unprepared I was to be a freaking coach.

Yes, I had skated all my life, and yes, I had been about to join the Olympic team before the accident, but that did not make me qualified to teach people how to do what I did—not a fucking snowball's chance in hell. Most of the time I was a robot just taking orders from my coaches. I had no idea how to motivate, lead, and teach to the caliber that athletes deserved from one of the most important people in their lives.

I sat on the first row of bleachers in the empty rink while I waited for Simon to meet with me. My knees knocked together under my dark blue leggings, partly from the chilly air, mostly from my nerves. I stared down at my feet, housed in the off-white skates I hadn't put on in far too long. It all felt so foreign and so right all at once. I was completely unnerved, yet in my element. It was a Jekyll and Hyde moment, two sides of me feverishly colliding—the old me trying to take back my life, the new me being scared shitless of it all.

Right as I was about to shoot off a text to Bray about not knowing if I was cut out for this, the metal door to my left swung open and Simon Abramson strode through. He was so graceful and impeccably dressed, practically sashaying as he smiled at me. "You must be Myla. Your brother speaks very highly of your talents, young lady."

I jumped to my feet and grabbed his outstretched hand, willing myself to not start gushing over the amazingly talented and accomplished skater in front of me. "Hopefully I can live up to all the hype."

"I'm sure you will. Are you ready to skate for me?"

I nodded. "What would you like to see?"

His grin turned a little playful as he pulled his lips together, tapping them with one finger while he thought for a moment. "Why don't you show me what you got? Your best, your favorite—just impress me, darling."

I took a deep breath and nodded. "Yeah. Sure."

It only took me a few seconds to get my skates laced up, slip the rubber guards off, and get out onto the rink. Right as my blade glided on the slick ice, I could feel panic start to build in my stomach. It was the first time I had even attempted to get back out there and there I was about to try to pull off a triple axel for the one and only Simon Abramson.

Fuck my life right now.

I started to slowly warm up and looked over to the smiling man as anticipation started to well up inside me. I felt like I was about to burst, but I needed that energy to pull off the jump. With a deep breath, I counted softly to myself.

One...

Two...

Three...

I was in the air, spinning, feeling freer than I had in over a year. I started to let my foot slide down to connect with the ice and...

Shit.

The cold from the hard ice smacked into my ass and back as my arms and legs went flying around me like I was some goddamned rag doll.

"I'm sure you didn't blow it." Brayden and I took our favorite seats on the back couch in Victory Coffee.

"I fell flat on my ass on jump number one. If Simon hires me, it will be a miracle for sure." The light hint of hazelnut in my coffee was starting to lift my spirits a bit.

"Oh, fuck," Brayden whispered, staring down the guy that had just walked through the door. He was tall and tattooed, and I knew him from somewhere but couldn't quite put my finger on it.

"Bray? Who is that?" My brother opened his mouth to answer but the subject of my inquiry started walking over to us with a crooked smirk spreading on his lips.

"Hey, rookie. Fancy seeing you here."

And then it clicked: Gavin Hayes—the best player and biggest asshat of the Otters.

"How ya doin', Gavin?" Brayden's chest puffed out as his glare narrowed.

Gavin shrugged. "Just living the dream." He glanced over at me, doing a quick onceover. "Aren't you going to introduce us?"

Brayden cleared his throat. "Gavin, this is Myla, my little sister."

I shook his hand. "Nice to meet you."

Before I could say anything back, a mother walked over with her young son. He was staring down at his feet as his mom whispered to him, "Don't be shy, Ryan."

"Excuse me." The little boy with bright yellow Converse and matching shirt was so nervous and adorable.

My brother and Gavin both looked at him, smiling. Brayden shimmied off the couch and onto his knee to get eye level with him "What's up, kid?"

The boy's face turned all kinds of red as a huge smile spread like wildfire. "Are you Cox and Hayes from the Otters?"

The mom put her hand on his shoulder. "Ryan is a huge hockey fan. He just started playing on a peewee team."

Gavin crouched down next to my brother. "Oh yeah? What position does your coach have you playing?"

Ryan started pulling at the bottom of his shirt. "I'm the left defender."

Gavin looked over his should to me. "Will you ask one of the baristas if they have a marker we could borrow?"

Trotting over, I got a Sharpie from a young worker that was frothing milk. "Who are they?" she asked, handing me the marker.

"They're players for the Otters." I smiled, glowing with pride from getting to experience a fan moment with my brother. It used to happen a lot with my dad when we were kids, but this was the first time it had happened to Brayden when I was with him. It hadn't really hit me until that moment that Brayden was a big deal and a hero to some people.

While Brayden and Gavin signed the little boy's shirt and chatted with him for a while, I stood back with his mother.

"I can't believe how sweet your boyfriend and his teammate are. Ry's whole room is decorated with Otters stuff from floor to ceiling. We just got him a huge stuffed Ollie and he sleeps with it every night."

I couldn't help the little laugh I let out. "Brayden is my brother, and we both had Otters décor littering our rooms growing up. Our dad and Gavin's played for the team, too."

She blushed a little. "Sorry, I didn't mean to assume."

Ryan scampered back over to his mom. "Mommy, look!" He was bouncing on his heels, pointing to the signatures on his bright shirt.

"Wow! Isn't that awesome!" She smiled sweetly. "Thank you. This made his year, I'm sure."

Six

Myla

One year later

Plopping down onto my light gray carpet, nail polish in hand, I glanced up at Simon, who was digging through my closet. I couldn't believe that in not even two years, I had gone from barely being able to walk to helping coach ice skating with one of my biggest idols, now turned best friend. It was all too surreal. I was still a little shaky on my skates when I pushed myself too hard or tried the more difficult jumps again, but every day I was getting stronger and Simon was pushing me just enough to get back in competing shape again.

"Myla, I just don't get it." Simon popped his hip out while staring at my walk-in closet full of clothes I never wore.

"Get what?" I looked up at my best friend, painting my toes a fiery red.

"I just cannot wrap my head around why in God's name you don't use any of these magnificent clothes!" He started digging until he found one of my favorite little black dresses and held it up in the mirror over himself. "If I had your boobs, butt, and long-ass legs, I'd rock this little number every day, all day!"

"I think you're missing the vagina too, Simon." I threw the pillow I had been leaning on at him and giggled. "I just don't have any reason to wear any of it any more. I'm pretty boring these days."

"You've always been boring, love. Sorry to break it to you, but you could be boring in style instead of the drab tracksuits and yoga pants you refuse to get out of."

He was right. Since everything had gone to shit the day of the accident, I had become boring as hell. The accident had stripped everything from me: my dreams, my liveliness, my confidence, my mom, everything.

"I just don't see the point anymore." I sighed, fixing the section of my cuticle I had just accidentally painted.

Simon huffed over, sat cross-legged in front of me, grabbed the nail polish out of my hands, and started to fix my terrible paint job on my toenails. "Look, my fortieth birthday is going to be at Gatsby's at nine on Wednesday. Let's break out a little cocktail number and let loose for a night, how does that sound?"

"Like you're going to push me out of my comfort zone."

"You better believe it, and it is going to be fabulous!" Simon's face lit up as anticipation of the upcoming festivities danced over his face.

"But what's the point of me even trying to go to a twenty-one-and-up martini bar? Did you forget I'm only twenty? Only a few more months, but who's counting?"

Simon's smile spread across his lips quickly as he stated very matter-of-factly, "Because it's my party and I rented the place out—my money, my rules, and one of those is that you're coming. And that's final! Simon says, after all, dear." He winked at me before laughing at himself.

I checked out Simon's amazing job with my polish and smirked. "Well, I guess I have plans Wednesday night then."

Brayden

I laced up my skates in the vacant locker room, thankful that no one else had shown up so I could have a little bit of private rink time before practice started in an hour. The ice was freshly cleaned and smooth under my blades.

It had been such a hard couple of years and I had no idea what I was doing. Being a player for my dream team was shocking, trying to take care of my sister was trying, dealing with my mother's death was not happening, and hating my father for being locked up was enraging. Everything rolled up into me loving the moments when someone pissed me off enough in the rink so I could knock the shit out of them and get rid of some of my pent up aggression.

Myla begged me to go talk to someone, which I knew would be for the best, but tough guy hockey players don't go to shrinks, and they sure as shit don't let people know they have feelings and emotions—a sign of weakness that would get my ass handed to me by even my own teammates.

I slammed my skates into the ice, marking and cutting it up. The cool air whisked by as the silence sank into my skin. Being alone was all too bittersweet; thoughts and questions boiled up from the darkest pits and I hated every minute of it, but then there were those quick moments of clarity and peace where I finally felt like I was the man my mother would be proud of and the role model my sister deserved.

One of the rink doors banged, pulling me away from my thoughts, and I growled when Gavin skated into my view. His cocky ass leer made me want to deck him, but he hadn't pushed me far enough to justify kicking his ass—*yet.*

"Hey, Cox. Trying to get in some extra skating practice so you stop looking like a damn ballerina out here?"

"Shut the hell up, Hayes. Don't you have another hour of kissing coach's ass before you start getting annoying?"

"Fuck you. That's no way to talk to your captain."

I flipped him off while bowing to him. "As you wish, your captain-ness."

"Jerk," he muttered under his breath.

It took everything in my power to not lay him out right there, but I wanted to keep my job and assaulting a teammate was frowned upon to say the least—let alone the captain and the fucking coach's son.

For the rest of the hour we practiced short stops and skating backward in complete silence. I really couldn't put my finger on it; I knew I hated Gavin, but I had no idea why. It wasn't that he was the coach's son; my father had also been a famous player back in the day. We both deserved to be there—he was one hell of a good player—but there was just something about him.

The hour went by and then it was time to actually practice. The rest of the team joined Gavin and me on the ice and it was business as usual. Even with all the sharp-tongued comments and obvious bad blood between Gavin and me, we were good at being teammates when it was all said and done. One thing I could really give both of us credit for was leaving most of our baggage off the ice.

Myla

"Girls!" I blew my whistle as loud as I could to get the elementary school-aged girls to pay attention to me.

"Girls, come on over here. We're going to practice skating backward today."

The ten tiny graceless kids shuffled their way over to me. It was adorable watching them waddle and try their best to be elegant. I was lucky; this group of peewees was way better behaved than the group I was in at their age. We used to make our coach's life a living nightmare, always getting hurt, never listening, trying to do moves that were way over our heads—I couldn't believe Mrs. Riley didn't give up on us after one week.

"Ok, Jess, you're up first." It was completely wrong, but I totally played favorites when it came to my kids, and Jessica Schwendeman was absolutely stealing my heart.

Her light brown hair was braided into two fish bones that ran all the way down her back, she had the cutest pink glasses, and her sweaters always matched them in some way. She had a drive and determination that was unseen in most adults. I could just tell that this little lady was going to really make something of herself; if it wasn't on the ice, it would be in the boardroom.

Her little fingers gripped mine. "But, Coach Myla, I've never skated backward before."

I held her hand a little tighter. "That's why I am going to teach you."

"Coach?" Jess asked as I started to slowly push her backward.

"Yeah sweetie?" She was being a trooper, but I

could see in her eyes how terrified she was.

Her cheeks turned a deeper shade as she bit her bottom lip. "Um, is it true that your brother plays for the Otters?"

She looked down at our skates.

"Yes, my brother is Brayden Cox. He plays right wing." Her crooked grin grew as crimson took over her entire face, moved down her neck, and even covered her ears. "Do you like hockey?"

She nodded her head feverishly. "I wanted to play hockey, but my mom said I would get hurt so I had to do this instead."

"Well, I'm glad you're here." Jessica's shaking ankles started to get noticeable.

Jessica's smile returned to her adorable face. "I'm glad I'm here too."

I started to bring her back over to the rest of the group. "Keep the pressure on the outside of your skates, and don't let your ankles roll inward."

I clapped, sending Jess back over to her friends. "Ok, who's next?"

Brayden

Taking my seat in the folding metal chair for the first time in years made my skin crawl. I gripped the cold shelf in front of me that led to the glass partition that would soon have my father on the other side.

Waiting for the guards to bring him in, my thoughts wandered back to being fifteen and the police banging on the door that Friday night while I sat on the couch with my mother and sister watching *My Cousin Vinnie* for the hundredth time.

"No, I'll get it." I grabbed my mom's hand as she tried to get up to see who was at the door. A voice called through the thick oak before I was even two steps away from the couch. "Police!"

With my mother and sister in tow, I opened the front door. "Officer? How can I help you?" I tried to lower my voice and sound like the man of the house I had become just a few weeks before.

"Son, is your mother home?" An older officer stood in front of me with his hands on his hips, and a younger redhead stood to his right, chewing on his gum like a cow.

"I'm right here." My mother shoved me out of the way, shooing me with her hands. "Bray, take your sister into the living room while I speak with the officers."

I nodded and grabbed Myla's shaking hand, turning toward our paused movie, but my feet didn't move. Every hair on my body stood on end as I listened to their conversation unravel.

"Ma'am, are you Mrs. Cox?"

My mother's voice broke as she said, "Yes, what's this about?"

"Is your husband Reggie Cox? Does he live here?"

"He is my husband, but he moved out a few weeks ago. I haven't heard from him in days."

"Mrs. Cox, your husband has been in an accident. He is at the hospital. We have every reason to believe he was intoxicated."

My mother gasped right as I turned around to watch her trembling body lean against the doorjamb. "Is he...?"

"He's stable, but he hit a car with a family in it. The two passengers passed on their way to the hospital and the driver is in critical condition. Ma'am, you might want to get your husband a lawyer."

The first thing I saw was how sunken my father's eyes were as he took his seat on the other side of the glass. I grabbed the black phone next to me and waited for him to get his to his ear.

"Hey, Pop. How's it going?" It was hard to look him in the eye. He had lost at least fifteen pounds since the last time I'd seen him. All the fight left in him had vanished. His dark eyes had receded into hollowed pits of nothingness. The life sentence was starting to get the better of my old man.

His voice was raspy as he choked out, "Fine. Same

shit, different day. What brings you down here, son? It's been a while."

"Good to see you too, Pop. I have some news to tell you. This isn't easy for me, but I figured it was your right to know...eventually, anyway."

I glared at a fly on the wall behind my father, trying to find the right words. Everything has gone to shit since the accident with Myla and Mom, and him being locked up was just the icing on the cake of it all. I didn't need him to be my dad, but it would have been nice to have one more person in my corner every once in a while.

"What's up, kid?"

"Well, it's Mom." I felt water trying to fill my eyes but I bit back my emotions when I saw that my father's expression hadn't changed. "She's gone."

There it was, the worry I had expected. He gripped the phone until his knuckles turned white and the little color he had left drained out of his cheeks as he asked, "What do you mean, *gone?*"

"Myla and Mom were on their way to visit you a while ago. A semi ran a stoplight and smashed into their car. Myla was in a coma for two days and had some pretty bad injuries. Mom didn't make it out of the car."

I felt like I had to spit the words out before they choked me. I hadn't explained the accident to anyone except Myla and this was the last time I planned on talking about it.

"Wait, they were coming here?"

I nodded and waited for the timeline to click in his head. All of a sudden his face went red, boiling crimson as his eyes shot daggers at me.

"It took you two fucking years to come here and tell me my wife is dead and my daughter almost met her maker too?"

All I could do was nod and grumble, "Ex-wife."

He jumped to his feet and screamed, "Guard!"

I yelled into the phone, "Nice seeing you, Pop. See you at your parole hearing next month."

I slammed the receiver down and walked away from my father as his cuffs were put on and he was escorted back to his cell.

Seven

Myla

Burrowing through my closet, I finally found the dress I had been looking for. I knew I needed a showstopper for Simon's birthday party to finally make him shut up about my usual attire.

After taking a shower and shaving my legs for the first time in weeks, I dug my makeup bag out and turned on my curling iron. Usually, I let my long blonde hair air dry into its normal straight layers, but that night I was going to pull out every trick in the book that I could flipping think of.

Doing my makeup and curling my hair, I finally started to feel like a girl again for the first time in years. I had been overly girly growing up, making sure not even one eyelash was out of place, but once my life changed, so did how much I cared about my appearance.

In my full-length mirror, I did a onceover. My curls were tight and holding well, super bouncy and cute. My makeup was simple and natural; I didn't want to go overboard. Since I hadn't really worn much makeup in over two years, the process called for baby steps for sure. My long dark blue chiffon dress was strapless and formfitting in all the right places. I topped it off with a really high pair of taupe pumps and a clutch to match.

This is going to be a really good night.

It was like a sigh of relief was coming over me. I saw the old me shining through just a little and it was a comforting feeling, like getting home after a long trip away and crawling into your own bed again.

The sound of the front door slamming startled me. "Brayden?" I called through my open bedroom door.

From down the stairs I heard a slurred, "Yeah, it's me."

Brayden's heavy footsteps thumped on each creaky step of our old home, making their way up to my room. I yanked the zipper to my dress up and smoothed it out right as his big, muscular figure filled my doorway.

"Going somewhere, sis?"

I looked at my brother in the reflection of the mirror over my dresser. "Uh huh." I mumbled, pulling my lips tight over my teeth, smearing on lip gloss. "It's Simon's birthday, so I'm going to meet him at a club on the Upper East Side. A cab will be here pretty soon. Wanna tag along?"

I could smell the copious amounts of alcohol Brayden had obviously just consumed from across my room and was silently hoping he would decline my offer. Slowly he made his way from leaning on my doorframe to sitting on my bed.

This cannot be good.

"Bray?"

He looked up at me, his normally bright amber eyes glossed over and a few days of stubble lining his jaw. He looked like a freaking train wreck. "Yeah sis?"

"Is everything okay? I thought practice was going to be running late. Shouldn't you still be at the rink?"

"Nope. Not this guy." He lazily tried to point at himself before his hand fell back into his lap.

I took a seat next to him on my bed. "What the hell happened this time?"

"I got sent home early." His words started to completely slur together.

"Ugh! Brayden! How badly did you hurt the other guy?"

"He hooked me right into the boards, so I tried to break his eye socket." As the words slowly slipped from his lips, he began to look more and more upset. His left eye started to close, just enough to show how fucking wasted he really was.

"It happens, man. You know that. Remember in high school when that guy broke your nose for blocking his shot?"

Brayden smirked a little. "Yeah, but that wasn't my

teammate, My. Coach is fuckin' pissed as all hell."

I patted him on the shoulder as his body swayed a bit. "I'm sure it wasn't as bad as you think. It will all blow over by the next practice."

Brayden leaned back on my bed, propping himself up by one elbow, and started laughing. "Yeah, I hope so. He is the coach's son though, so he might hold a grudge on this one."

"Holy shit, Bray. You're fighting with Gavin Hayes? He's the freaking best defender you have and you're pissing him off?" I hated getting into my brother's team business but hockey was in both of our blood and I couldn't always hold my tongue on how stupid he could be most of the time.

"I went to visit him today. It was bad. That bastard sperm donor of ours." My brother's words hit my heart with a sledgehammer.

"What the hell, Brayden? You promised! If we were going to tell him, we'd do it together." I took a few slow breaths to cool my building temper.

"Yeah, I know, but I didn't want you to have to see him like that. He's not the same person. He's not our dad anymore."

I started to pace around my room, trying to level myself out. I knew my brother was trying to do the right thing and protect me, but protecting me from my own father—that was a little more than I could handle. "We'll talk about this in the morning." I seethed as I heard a horn blare from outside my window. "I won't be home until late. Sleep off that whiskey, Bray. You smell like you brought the bar home with you."

Grabbing my purse and shoving my lip gloss in, I leaned over and kissed my big brother on the cheek. He whispered, "Love ya," then fell back on my bed and immediately started snoring.

Fucking perfect.

"Myla, oh thank God! You came and you look fabulous!" Practically singing, Simon grabbed my hand and twirled me around a few times before he took me into his arms. "Come, I have tons of people to introduce you to."

The club was bustling with wall-to-wall people dancing, laughing, and drinking. Everyone kept grabbing Simon to try to get him to dance, chat, or do shots with them. It was my first time in an actual night club, and the bright flashing lights, the loud pounding bass, and the exorbitant number of people grinding on each other was all a lot to take in while being whisked around by my arm and shaking hands with everyone we passed.

"Adam!" Simon screamed over to a tall ginger that was getting a cocktail from the bar. His light gray button-down clung to his arms, shoulders, and chest, his face was lightly dusted with freckles, his long, dark red hair was pulled back into a bun, and he had a thick well-kept beard surrounding a gorgeous, toothy grin. I stopped dead. This guy was one of the most handsome men I had ever seen. I mean come on, a mun? *Yes, please.*

"Simon, how are you?" They shook hands before Simon led the tall drink of water over to me.

"This is one of my dearest friends, Myla. Adam was one of my students when he was in high school."

Adam turned a thousand shades of red as he took my hand. "It's a pleasure to meet you."

"So, you're a figure skater?" We took seats at the bar. I looked around for Simon but he had gotten lost in the crowd of guests.

Adam shook his head. "I tried it out when I broke my wrist pretty badly playing varsity hockey. How do you know Simon?"

"I'm one of his assistant coaches."

He waved over to the bartender. "What're you drinking, Myla?"

I blushed a little. "Just water, thanks."

The bartender handed me a plastic cup with a lemon on the rim.

"Not drinking tonight?" He smiled, drinking from

his martini glass. He looked so sophisticated and I felt like a little girl—cue nervousness and extreme awkwardness.

I giggled a little, trying to mask my nerves. "I don't really drink."

"Ah. You're one of *those* types of athletes." I strained to ignore the condescending undertone of the statement, but it got the better of me.

"What do you mean one of *those?*" I was trying to play coy; I had never flirted with an older guy before. With all the skating practice I did during high school, there was no room for flirting, or dating at all. The longest relationship I'd ever had had only consisted of about two months of barely communicating through texts, two dinner-and-a-movie dates, and one failure of a sexual encounter—super lame.

"It's a good thing you're that disciplined to not drink. You're probably in great shape." His eyes traveled down my bare legs and back up to my cleavage. In seconds, I felt completely exposed.

"I guess you could say that. I've actually never had a drink in my life."

Adam nearly choked. Coughing and grabbing his chest, he exclaimed, "What?"

I shook my head, smiling. "Nope, never touched a drop. My brother drinks enough for the both of us, to be honest. I've never even been interested in it."

"So how does a nice girl like you wind up working

for a crazy-ass like Simon?" Adam waved to the bartender for another drink. "Perfect gin martini stirred with the dirty ice back, please."

His drink sounded so refined and he was freaking dreamy—and probably way out of my league. I guessed he was at least in his mid-twenties and the Rolex he kept flicking on his wrist was just the right amount of flashy. Brayden would refer to him as a pompous-ass motherfucker, but there was something so James Bond about Adam without being completely clean cut and falling into the tall, dark, and handsome category. He had the tall and handsome part nailed down, and his long red hair and beard were extremely sexy to me.

"I was a figure skater until I was in a car accident. You know the saying *Those who can't do, teach*? Well that's me to a T at this point."

His warm hand landed on my leg, making shivers shoot up my spine.

Is this guy being too forward?

Is this fucking normal?

Act cool.

Don't let your age show.

"Myla!" Simon scream-slurred in my ear. Adam removed his hand, smiling at our friend as Simon hooked an arm around each of our necks. "I'm just so glad you two are hitting it off. I knew you would. I just freaking knew it!"

"You always know best, Coach." Adam winked at me.

"Simon says!" Simon yelled at the top of his lungs before leaning on the bar to bark his drink order at the bartender.

"Is he always like this when he's out?"

Adam pursed his lips together. "Honestly, I wouldn't know. This is my first time out with him since I moved back to the city."

"Oh, when was that?"

"A few weeks ago. My company just absorbed another right here in Manhattan and when the board members suggested the move, I couldn't turn it down."

"So what is it that you do?" I rested my elbow down onto the bar top, right into something extremely sticky. It icked me out to no end but I kept a straight face, sliding my arm back and trying to wipe it off without drawing attention to myself.

Goodness, you're such a mess!

Luckily, Adam was too into telling me about himself to notice my embarrassing situation. "In college I started an insurance software company, just trying to make ends meet while I was supporting myself through school. Turns out, there is a lot more money in that than I could have even hoped. I'm lucky to say I have done pretty well for myself and since then, I have always been my own boss."

"That's incredible." *What was an accomplished business mogul doing in a bar talking to a nobody like me?*

"Eh, it has its moments. It's not the most interesting job in the world, but running my own company is something I have always wanted to do. What are your dreams, Myla?"

I wanted to say so many other things than what came out of my mouth. I wanted to say that I wished I had been able to go to the Olympics, that I wanted to be a professional figure skater, that I never imagined being washed up before my nineteenth birthday, but all that came out was, "I'll let you know when I figure out what they are."

"Sounds good to me. So do you mind if I ask how old you are?"

"Isn't that very ungentlemanly of you?" *Deflection—perfect.*

He chuckled a little. "I guess you're right. My apologies, my lady." He bowed his head and I burst out laughing.

"I'm twenty. And you are?"

His face never wavered. Hopefully my age wasn't going to be a problem for him. "I am twenty-six."

"Does my age bother you?" I was so inexperienced compared to him in just the simple game of life. He'd been to college, started a company, made a crap-load of money before his twenty-fifth birthday, and I was barely seeing the outside of a skating rink for most of my life.

His hand traveled up to touch my shoulder as he shook his head. "No. Should it?"

"Not in the slightest."

The tiny, playful smirk that landed on his lips was so damn enthralling. "Good."

"It's getting late. I should probably call it a night."

He pulled out his wallet, taking a business card out and folding it into my hand. "When can I see you again?"

I put his card into my clutch, smiling. "Sometime?" *I think I am getting the hang of this flirting thing.*

"Well, why don't you write your number down and let me call you soon so we can figure something out."

I scribbled my number onto a bar napkin for Adam. "Sorry, I'm not important enough to have business cards."

Putting the napkin in his wallet, he laughed a little. "I'll be the judge of how important you are, and having business cards is totally overrated. I'd much rather see your handwriting on a bar napkin; it's one of a kind, not a dime a dozen."

EIGHT

Gavin

Slam. I threw her hard against the wall, pressing my chest against hers, knotting my fingers into her messy hair.

She tasted like white zinfandel and cigarettes, two of the most loathsome tastes in the entire world, but she was hot.

She'd do for one night.

Pulling her leg over my hip, I ran my fingers up her tight skirt, finding her lack of underwear hilarious.

Bar slut.

I knew I needed to stop this one-night stand crap, knew I craved companionship, but during the season, with my hectic schedule and being on the road so much, dating was not in the cards.

I kissed her perfume-covered neck. *Fuck.* Chanel No. 5—the same shit Marsheila used to wear. There I was trying to fight through the memories when all I wanted was to just get a nut off and pass out. *Is that too much to fucking ask for?* It had been over two years since I was left at that altar and she was still plaguing my mind.

What in the ever-loving fuck?

Get a goddamned grip.

She moaned. "I can't believe I am at Gavin Hayes' apartment."

"Believe it sweetheart, this is going to be a night you will never forget."

In the dim light of the apartment, I could barely make out her skin tone or actual hair color, but who the hell cares about that shit when it really comes down to it? I was a firm believer that having a type when it came to women totally stacked the deck in the wrong favor.

Fuck it.

I threw her over my shoulder, arm hooked right under her tiny ass cheeks. *What was her name? Kayla, I think her name was Kayla, or was that the brunette I was talking to at the beginning of the night? Damn it.* The manhattans were starting to play games with my memory already.

Giggling, her breathy voice came from behind me. "Where are we going?"

"The shower," I stated sharply as I rounded the corner into the master bathroom.

She wiggled a little in my arms. "But, wait! I don't want to get my hair wet." The whine that laced her tone was fucking annoying. *I'm going to have to fill that hole fast so she shuts the fuck up.*

"Quite frankly, my dear, I don't give a flying rat's fucking ass."

Setting her down on the bathroom sink, I made quick work of unzipping her tight skirt and yanking her lacey blouse over her head.

I nipped at her neck. *Yup. We need to get rid of that stench.*

Getting down to my boxers, I turned on the shower.

"Seriously, Gavin. I don't want to get my hair wet." She was still on the granite counter, swinging her legs like a damn teenager.

I pulled open my medicine cabinet, flicking a hair tie at her. "Then pull it up and I'll stand in the water, babe."

She chewed on her lip as I took in her features. Long tan legs, long dirty blonde hair, a decent face, a sweet smile, ice blue eyes—she was decently cute. I had done better, but I sure as shit had done way worse. She was skinnier than I usually went for, almost anorexic-looking skinny, not the in shape, athletic, toned women I typically wanted. I had to work out hard, and I liked when my chick could understand that.

I slipped off my boxers and watched her eyes dart to my junk. Why do girls always have to check it out?

Don't they understand the phrase *a grower not a shower?*

She bit her bottom lip. "I want it."

A quick wink was all I could muster. I was totally half-assing that shit; usually I would have been rock hard already, but my mind was just not in the game at all. "Then get your cute ass into this shower."

I opened the door and walked in. The warm water felt amazing; there was something so peaceful about washing the day away.

"Do you want to know my name?" she asked as she sheepishly shuffled into the far side of the massive shower.

Fuck. Please be right.

"Kayla, right?"

Her face lit the fuck up like the fourth of July. "I didn't think you would remember."

I brushed her shoulders softly, pouring a little bit of water over the areas where I smelled that awful perfume. "How could I forget the same of someone so pretty? I'm not a complete ass."

Kayla giggled, an annoying, high-pitched schoolgirl giggle that made my skin crawl. "That's not what your reputation says, but I like surprises."

I wanted to bark at her, tell her I'd show her how big of an ass I could really be, but my actions were going to scream way louder than words ever could.

The beast in me came out. Plain and simple, I was

primal.

Pushing her body against the cold tiled wall with one hand, I started to stroke my growing cock with the other. "You want this?"

Her little doe eyes batted while she nodded.

"Then take it." My hand on her shoulder forced her to kneel. I slapped the tip onto her lips. "Open."

Water started to spray off my body onto hers as she opened her mouth wide enough for me to enter. Grabbing her messy bun, I thrust deep into the back of her throat. Listening to her cough was more invigorating than it should have been.

Pulling her mouth away, Kayla looked up at me. "Let me do it."

I smiled, waiting a second as she gently licked the head of my dick. "No. Now open up like a good little slut or I am going to make you wish you had listened to me the first time."

Her lips parted while I read the apprehension across her face. *If she didn't want to play the game, she shouldn't have gotten in the cab.*

It was so frustrating taking a chick home that didn't actually know how to suck a guy off. I mean how hard could it really be? I wasn't really the teaching type, but I was going to get off somehow, and face-fucking was the way it needed to happen that night.

Gripping her hair again, I thrust in a little gentler

than before. "Just keep that mouth open and I will take care of the rest." Her eyes locked with mine as tears started to form at the corners. "Squeeze my leg if gets to be too much for you."

I knew that even if I was hurting her, it was going to take a lot for her to tap out after I had put her in her place. I let my mind trip through some of the better fucks I had had recently and felt my dick start to twitch. Pulling out, I started to stroke my cock, letting hot come pepper her reddened cheeks and spread over her tits.

Grabbing the washcloth from behind me, I wiped her off as she started to get back onto her feet.

Her red nails glided down my abs as she traced the O in the *Ominous* tattoo right over my boxer line. "My turn."

I titled my head to the side, smirking while I fought the laughter that was about to spew out of my mouth. "Oh no, honey. It's time for you to get the heck out of my place."

NINE

Myla

Bang.

Bang.

Bang.

In a sleepy daze, I barely realized that someone was knocking on my bedroom door.

"Myla?" Brayden yelled through the thick wooden door. "Myla, get up and get dressed, I have a surprise for you."

Squinting, I could barely make out the blaring red numbers on my alarm clock. "Bray, go back to bed, it's eight in the morning on a Saturday. Fucking enjoy the day off for once in your life."

The clicking of him picking my lock with a bobby pin got my ass to shoot right out of bed. "Fine. I'm up. Don't break my lock."

I flung the door open to find my brother completely dressed and holding my favorite sweater, waiting for me. "Hurry up, sis. We have to get a move on."

I went into my closet, shutting the door to get dressed. Yanking on a pair of jeans and almost busting my ass from getting my toes stuck in one of the rips, I couldn't help but be a little excited. It had been forever since my brother and I had spent more than a few hours together and usually it was over a rushed meal or on the rare occasion that Brayden had a little down time between practices. With opening day right around the corner, it was hard to believe he wasn't at the rink working on his skating speed.

"So what are we doing?" I pulled a tank top on and threw my hair into a bun. "Do I need makeup?"

Brayden was sitting on my bed, checking his phone. "No, you're fine just the way you are. It's going to be so pretty out today. You're going to love this." His face was all lit up, scrolling through something on his screen.

"So do I even get a clue as to what you're about to get me into?"

He gave me a quick wink before jumping to his feet. "Nope."

Training into the city was one of my favorite things

to do in the fall. The leaves were golden red and the temperature holding in the mid-sixties was perfect.

"We're going to Central Park, aren't we?" I nudged Brayden, who was dazed and staring out the window.

"I told you this is all going to be a surprise, My. Can't you just let this be exciting and let me do something nice for my sister?"

Once we got off at Penn Station, we started walking right for the park. "I knew it!" I hooked my arm with my brother's and practically skipped the entire way.

"We're just about there."

I could hear dogs barking, which wasn't completely out of the ordinary for Central Park on a Saturday, but this was more than normal for sure. Rounding the corner, I could see tons of tents bustling with people walking around with puppies on leashes, in cages, and in little playpens all over.

"What is this?" The octave of excitement my voice reached was probably only audible for the dogs.

"It's an adoption festival. I figured with opening day coming up and my schedule becoming jam-packed for the rest of the season, a puppy would help keep you company."

I literally shrieked, grabbing Brayden's arm and jumping up and down like a five-year-old.

"Is this real life?"

While laughing, Brayden grabbed my hand, leading

me over to a crate with the most adorable beagle puppies. "So, what kind do you want?"

I scanned the area, trying to find one that was going to catch my eye. All of a sudden I heard a howl and knew right away what we needed to get. "Huskies!"

Dragging my brother to the other end of the row of tents, I locked eyes with the most adorable brown and white fluff ball rolling around with another husky in a playpen. I marched right over to the table where a pretty blonde was sifting through some paperwork.

Her face lit up when she saw us. "Brayden, right?" She squinted her eyes at my brother as he scratched the back of his head for a second.

When the light bulb switched on in my brother's brain, his face matched her excitement. "Karla?"

She started to blush as she beamed at my brother. "You remembered."

"How could I forget? Myla, this is one of your nurses from the ICU. She saved me the first night you were in there, took my number and made sure I had some shred of sanity through it."

I shook her hand. "It's so great to meet you."

Karla came out from behind the table, wrapping me in a huge hug. "You have no idea how amazing it is to meet you and see how amazing you're doing." Her unadulterated joy was palpable as we held each other for a few seconds. It felt like I was hugging a long-lost friend.

When she pulled away, Karla looked over to Brayden. "What brings you two to the park today?"

Brayden rubbed the back of his neck, fixing his Yankees hat. "We're here to get Myla a puppy. Do you work for the ASPCA or something now?"

Shaking her head, Karla started to walk us over to the husky puppies. "No, I just volunteer with them when they do events on my days off. I love helping people but I have a soft spot for puppies in need for sure."

"Oh God, Bray! Look how cute that one is!" I started bouncing on my heels.

Karla pointed to the same one that had caught my eye earlier. "She's a cutie and a handful, definitely needs to go to a home where someone will have tons of time to play with her. Want me to take her out so you can get to know her a bit?"

Brayden

Watching Myla run around in the grass and fallen leaves with the puppy I was sure what we were about to bring home was absolutely amazing. I had been so worried about leaving her for long periods during the season, I knew this was what both of us needed—me, for peace of mind, and her, for a real companion to focus on. It was perfect.

"So, how has it been going for you two? It's been what, a few years now?" Karla was even prettier than I remembered. Her natural dirty blonde hair was longer now, she had bright red lipstick on, and her ass looked amazing in her skintight jeans. I couldn't help but notice how stunning she was even in a t-shirt that had a few dog butts on it and said *Money can buy lots of things, but it doesn't wiggle its butt every time you come home.*

"Yeah, just about. We're still getting back to normal, but we're doing great for the most part. How's everything at Flushing?"

Karla was filling up the water bowl in the playpen. "Same shit, different day, I guess. I'm not working nights anymore, so that's a plus."

I scrolled through my contacts. "You know; I still have your number. Maybe I could call you sometime? Take you out for coffee or something. I never properly thanked you for saving me that night."

Sweetly, she looked up at me. "You don't have anything to thank me for, but I would love to hang out with you sometime."

Myla started to jog back over to us with the puppy in her arms. "Bray! She's perfect."

"Awesome, sis. This was way easier than I thought it was going to be."

Karla started to go over the adoption paperwork with us and within twenty minutes, our new puppy was ready to head home.

"Thanks!" Myla grabbed both Karla and me, squeezing the ever-loving shit out of us. "This is going to be the best ever."

I glanced down at Myla; the spark that had reignited in her had been long missed. "I'm glad you're happy, sis. Now let's get this little girl some fun stuff!"

Karla was beaming, helping Myla put a new collar and leash on our puppy. "This will do just fine until you can get her something special. Do you know what you're going to name her?"

Biting her lip, Myla stood in thought for a second, tapping her finger to her chapped lips. "Oh, I know! Seven! After Seven James."

I furrowed my brow. "From a book?" It was the only explanation I could think of.

Myla nodded. "From the *Hers* series by Dawn Robertson. Seven is a total badass with a huge heart. It's perfect."

Karla nodded. "I can totally see Seven's spunk in this little pup! Perfect name!"

"You've read the series?"

Karla's smile widened. "Dawn Robertson opened my eyes to how awesome erotic romance can actually be!"

Myla practically jumped with joy. "Oh man, me too! Did you hear that *Ryker* is coming out soon?"

I let the girls chat about their smutty book obsession while I played tug of war with Seven using a rope toy Karla was going to let us take home. It was refreshing seeing Myla get excited about so many things in such a short period of time. I missed that side of my sister; usually she was excited twenty-four-seven, and hopefully this was the start of getting all that back.

TEN

Myla

Seven was sleeping at the foot of my bed and snoring softly as I pet her fluffy head with my big toe. I could hear Brayden's shower running, which thankfully meant it was getting close to breakfast time—the noises my stomach was making sounded like a swamp thing had taken up residence in my gut.

Right as I was about to roll out of bed, my phone dinged with a text.

Adam: Good morning, beautiful.

Seeing a man, I thought was way out of my league call me beautiful first thing in the morning was a thrilling feeling that I, sadly, had never felt before.

Me: Morning. How're you?

Adam: Doing well. Just wondering when I am going to get to see you again.

Me: My schedule is pretty wide open.

Adam: Perfect. Dinner tomorrow night?

Me: Sounds like a plan.

Adam: Great. I'll make reservations and give you the details later.

Me: Awesome! Can't wait.

Adam: Neither can I.

Seven started to whimper that the door. "Ok girl, let's get you outside before you have another accident in the house and Brayden decides to make good on his threats to take you back to the shelter."

I threw my robe on and shuffled into my fluffy slippers, picking my new puppy up into my arms. The first week with her had been a learning experience for all of us—to say the least—but we were getting the hang of it. She was finally starting to listen to her name and picking up on my routine. Crate training wasn't going well, but slow and steady was going to win that race for sure.

Setting Seven down on the back steps that led to our small fenced yard, I heard Brayden tinkering in the kitchen.

"Bray? Can you start the coffee?" I called through the screen door as Seven hopped down the wooden steps, rushing into the yard for her morning pee.

"Way ahead of you!" Brayden replied, coming out to join me with two cups of steaming coffee in hand.

The smell of pumpkin spice wafted into my nostrils. "You're the fucking best, bro."

"Oh trust me, I know. Egg whites?"

I licked the sweet coffee from my lips before responding. "Yes, please."

The rest of my Sunday was spent lazily reading on our back deck, letting Seven get all her crazy puppy energy out frolicking around the backyard. The crisp fall air caressed my body as I flipped the pages faster and faster. I needed to know if Nutter was actually as crazy as he seemed and if Bender was really going to be the hero he didn't think he could be. I swooned at M. Stratton's words as the hours ticked by. Right before I was about to hit the big climax that had been building for the last few chapters, my phone started vibrating in my pocket.

I cleared my throat before answering the call. "Hey, Simon. How're you?"

His flamboyant personality rang in his voice through the phone. "I'm great. Want to grab a bite after work tomorrow? I feel like we haven't had a date night in forever."

"It's been too long! But I have an actual date tomorrow night with Adam. Rain check?"

His voice hit an entirely new octave as he shrilled.

"You what? That is so fantastic!"

I bit my lip; I was starting to get nervous about the entire thing. "Simon, I just don't know if I should go out with Adam."

I heard a heavy sigh come from the other end of the line. "I thought you liked him. I could tell he was totally into you."

"It's not that I don't want to, I'm just nervous." I got up from my chair, starting to pace around the backyard as Seven trotted behind me.

"Nervous? You two hit it off so well the other night. You'll have a great time." Simon started to chomp on something crunchy in my ear.

"Eating celery again?" It was Simon's addiction and it was so freaking odd to me. *How can someone eat celery all the time? Gross.*

"Don't change the subject. Why are you nervous, my dear?"

"Ugh. He's just so much older than me, probably way more experienced. What if I disappoint him?"

"Oh, honey, no one is telling you that you have to sleep with him on the first date. Go to dinner, enjoy yourself a bit, get dropped off, and go in for a goodnight kiss like a normal girl."

A gentle tap came on my hotel room door. I checked the clock—it was already well past our lights-out time. With having a competition in the morning, I was reluctant to answer the door, but I had a pretty good feeling who it was going to be.

Tommy was standing in my doorway with his goofy ass smile and thick-framed glasses, making me melt within seconds. "Come on, My, just let me in for a bit?"

Whispering, I moved out of the way so he could enter my hotel room. "You know if Ms. Riley catches us we won't be able to skate tomorrow."

Breaking the rules had never been a strong suit of mine.

Sitting down on the end of the bed, Tommy looked up at me with his crooked smirk that made me weak in the knees. "Is it a crime that I want to spend a little bit of time with my girl?"

I had never been anyone's anything before—cue the swooning feels and butterflies crashing.

"No, I guess not." I took a seat next to him, fixing my gaze on the blank television screen as my nerves started to get the better of me.

"Are you ready for tomorrow?" Tommy put his hand on my knee. "You looked awesome today during practice."

I turned to him. "You really think so?"

He scooted a little closer to me, close enough that I could feel his hot breath on my shoulder. "Yeah. You're going to kill it tomorrow."

And with that our lips were touching. I had never even really been alone with a guy that wasn't family. A rush came over me that I couldn't explain at all. I was a mess of excitement, nerves, flutters, and jitters all rolled into me having no idea what the fuck to do. Being seventeen and completely inexperienced wasn't unheard of in the competitive sports world, but I was still embarrassed by it.

Tommy's hand started to travel its way up my thigh while our lips were still locked together.

"Tommy, I don't know if this is a good idea."

He put a finger over my lips, shushing me. "Don't worry babe, I'll be gentle."

Within minutes, we were both naked under the covers with his hard cock pushing into my stomach as he kissed down my neck. "You're so beautiful, Myla. Since the moment I met you, I've been thinking about this happening."

Tommy's hot sticky body was making it hard for me to breath as he slowly started to rub the head of his dick over my clit.

"Do you have a condom?" I breathed into his ear, trying to make it sound as sexy as possible.

Reaching over, he grabbed his jeans and pulled out a small wrapper. "Of course, babe."

He put on the rubber and slid his slender manhood into me without warning. Euphoria was as far from the truth as I could ever imagine. He thrust a few times, moaning loudly as I pretended to enjoy the encounter.

No more than a minute or two passed before Tommy was shuddering on top of me, dripping with sweat and panting. "Oh God, Myla. You felt amazing."

And that was when I learned what a two-pump chump really was.

ELEVEN

Gavin

"So, my mom told me you were the captain of your team. Is that like, a big deal, or somethin'?"

I tried to not roll my eyes. The chick clearly wanted to be there even less than I did, and that was a freaking shock. I needed to stop letting my mother set me up on blind dates with the pretentious daughters of her tennis friends from the country club.

"Yes. I am the captain of the Otters. And what is it that you do for work again?" I continued pushing the pieces of lettuce around my chilled plate.

My date was pretty enough, way better than any of the other women I had been set up with over the last year. Her huge tits—which had probably been a college graduation present—were popping out of her low-cut blouse as she twirled a long curl between her fingers.

"I'm a paralegal working for my father's firm. It boring, but temporary." I couldn't help but stare at the bright pink lipstick that was clinging to her front tooth. I knew I should say something, but it was more entertaining to see how long it would last there; I had to have some form of fun on this crappy date.

"Why temporary?" I had never been great at small talk; if the conversation didn't flow naturally, why force it?

She slurped her chardonnay, making me want to yell *Check!* at the top of my lungs. "I'm planning on being a housewife."

There we have it ladies and gents, the deal breaker of the fucking century. I was all for my future wife staying home if that was what she really wanted to do, but for it to be an ambition in life was just plain irksome.

The rest of the evening was as painful as the beginning of the date was. The only win was her going home in her own cab, leaving me to head to the bar for a nightcap with Sean and Jordan.

"Here's to another epic fail in Mrs. Hayes' matchmaking career." Sean raised his glass to mine and Jordan held her stomach from laughing so hard. "At least this one had a nice set of twins on her."

"Sean, don't be gross." Jordan shot a sharp look over at him before turning to me. "You know, Gavin, one of these days you're going to have to tell your poor mom to just cut her losses and realize good breeding isn't all it's cracked up to be." Jordan was completely right, but I just didn't know how to say no to my mother. She had this weird way of being able to talk me into anything.

I glanced around the restaurant bar that Jordan was guest bartending at for the next month. "How's it been going at this place?"

Jordan was barley tall enough to reach over the whole bar. She started shaking a drink over her shoulder. "They're paying me well to get their staff in shape, so I can't complain. I like the change in pace."

"Hey McBee! Over here!" Sean started waving to a chick I had never seen before.

"Who's that?" I pointed over at the semi-tall chick with an awesome rack and bouncing maroon curls that was waving back at Sean as he walked over to greet her.

I looked over at Jordan, who gave me a quick shrug. "Fuck if I know."

"Guys, this is Jessica, my new partner."

Her bright blue eyes lit up as she shook our hands and took a seat in between Sean and me.

We all made small talk for a while, getting to know Sean's new partner.

"You know; this is the first time Sean has introduced us to someone he works with." I took a long gulp from my Manhattan.

Jessica's face lit up and she nudged Sean's arm with her elbow. "I guess I made a good first impression."

"You ain't half bad, rookie. First partner I have had

that is at least entertaining to talk to."

Right then my attention was diverted to the door as it was opening. A well-dressed guy was holding it for one of the most gorgeous women I had ever seen in my life. I couldn't put my finger on it, but I knew her from somewhere. Her long blonde hair was bouncing with loose curls as she glided into the restaurant on heels. Her legs went on for miles, leading up to an ass that was perfectly sculpted in a tight pencil skirt that was about to make my heart stop.

As I picked my jaw off of the floor, Jordan threw an olive at me. "Hey, creeper. See a ghost or something?"

The woman gave me a quick knowing smile as her date guided her over to the host stand with his hand on the small of her back.

"I feel like I know her from somewhere. Did she go to school with us?" I couldn't look away. I watched as her hips swayed all the way to the white linen-covered table. Her date was good, even pulled out the chair for her.

"Gavin, she's a little younger than we are—though I'm sure you would have hit that in high school anyway."

I shrugged. "Maybe she just has one of those faces."

Myla

Adam had me swooning from the first moment I

met him in front of the restaurant.

He helped me out of my cab and I realized I was fifteen minutes late. "I hope you haven't been waiting too long. Brayden was being a pain in my ass with his whole *big brother needs to ask a million questions about what his little sister is doing going out all dolled up* bullshit."

Adam just gave me a little grin while opening the door for me. "You're well worth any wait, my dear."

Walking in, I couldn't help but get a rush of excitement; it was my first real date, after all. The décor was impeccable, from the white linen tablecloths to the marble flooring and the servers wearing bowties. It wasn't that I wasn't used to going to nice restaurants, it was just a really exciting moment for me—everything seemed so much fancier with me on Adam's arm.

He was dressed to kill in a charcoal gray blazer, blue button-down that brought out his eyes, beard perfectly trimmed, and hair pulled up in an adorable mun—it was perfect.

As we were being escorted to our table, I could feel that someone was staring at me. I squinted over at the bar on the far side of the restaurant to see none other than Gavin Hayes posted up with a few people, glaring at me with a dazed and confused kind of look.

Adam pulled my seat out for me. "Do you know him?"

I peeked over my shoulder at Adam as he put my

napkin in my lap for me. *What a freaking gentleman!* "He's one of my brother's friends. He probably doesn't recognize me; we've only met a few times."

I hadn't told Adam about my brother being a player for the Otters; I wanted him to like me for me, not because my brother was kind of famous.

"Ah, I see." He took his seat across the table from me.

Our server was tableside within seconds. "Can I start you two off with some beverages?"

Adam handed the man the wine list. "Bring us a bottle of the BV Georges de Latour Private Reserve Cabernet Sauvignon and sparkling mineral water to start."

Our server came back with the bottle and filled both of our wine glasses for us. I whispered, "Adam, you know I'm only twenty."

He rolled his eyes and a little smile flashed on his lips. "One glass isn't going to kill you. Besides, for your first drink, it should be something this perfect."

"What do you mean perfect?" I pretended like I knew what I was doing, swirling the wine in my glass and smelling it, like I had seen in the movies. I felt like a low-class fool trying to pull the wool over Adam's eyes, but he seemed too wrapped up in explaining the wine to me to notice.

"This wine is my favorite because it boasts

exceptionally powerful yet elegant flavors. The highly saturated aromas and expansive, richly textured zests brim with deep blackberry and cassis expression. Layered nuances of espresso bean, crushed anise seed, bay leaf, violet, and toasted oak contribute complexity to the sumptuous dark-fruit character."

Well, la di da.

He's a nice guy that likes wine, not a complete snob, right?

I was hoping Adam was just trying to impress me—and in a way it was working—but I couldn't help but have an overwhelming urge to roll my eyes at him.

"I didn't realize how complicated wine flavors could be." I took a sip and wanted to vomit right on the spot. Apparently, I did not like red wine at all.

"My father owns a vineyard in Millbrook. I grew up on this stuff. Most of the time I think it's ostentatious, but I do love a good cab." Adam swirled his wine, taking a deep breath in. "There's just something so sexy about the way the flavors play on your tongue. You probably think I'm crazy."

I took another sip, trying my best to not purse my lips at the bitter, strong flavors. "No, I think it's good to be passionate about things you enjoy."

Adam reached across the table, taking my hand in his. "I am really glad we're doing this. It's been a long time since I met a girl I really felt a connection with."

Melt. Swoon. Cue the violins and flying doves.

After Adam ordered for us and we did the basic small talk, I was at a loss for words. It wasn't that the night wasn't going well, I just realized how little I had to talk about.

"I feel like you've lived this incredible, exciting life and I am just so boring." I took a bite of my herb-crusted salmon, trying to think of something else to talk about.

"Are you kidding? You've done so much. Tell me more about working with Simon. It must be entertaining, to say the least."

Spearing a baby carrot with my fork, I looked up to see Gavin walking toward the bathroom. "Hold that thought, I need to use the little girl's room."

I folded my napkin and made my way over to the hallway that led to the restrooms. "Gavin?" I called over.

He whipped around, the biggest smile on his face. "I knew you looked familiar!" He gave me a little hug.

I giggled. "You have no idea who I am, do you?"

He rubbed the back of his neck for a second. "Embarrassingly, I cannot put my finger on it, which is surprising because I don't usually forget such a pretty face."

"I'm Myla Cox." I saw the wheels turn in Gavin's head as it all clicked.

"Oh man! We met at that coffee shop! You're Brayden's sister."

I pointed to the door to the ladies' room. "Well, it was nice seeing you."

Gavin's smile was pretty invigorating. "Hopefully I'll run into you again sometime."

"As long as you remember me next time." I gave Gavin a quick wink before ducking into the bathroom.

The night went by smoothly enough with choppy conversation and delicious food.

Not bad for my first date.

"Thanks for a lovely evening." Adam pulled the car over to the curb in front of my house, grabbing my hand. "I hope to see you again soon." His lips brushed the back of my hand and I started to turn into a puddle of goo in his front seat.

I gave his hand a quick squeeze before starting to open the door. "I had a great time." I leaned over and gave him a peck on the cheek. "Text me later?"

He brushed my cheek with the back of his fingers. "You can count on that."

Lying in bed, I was reeling from the amazing date. I couldn't believe I could feel that comfortable with a guy so quickly. There was just something so nice about being able to talk to someone that was really engrossed in what I had to say, even when I was struggling to keep the conversation interesting.

Pulling Seven up into my arms, I curled up to read a text that had just come through.

> **Adam: I know they say you're supposed to wait a few days to text a lady after an amazing date, but I just couldn't help it**
>
> **Me: I had a great night too, thanks again for an awesome dinner**
>
> **Adam: You're welcome. Do you like hockey?**
>
> **Me: Yes, would be an understatement**
>
> **Adam: I have two tickets to tomorrow night's game. You want to go with me?**

Brayden hated when I went to his games, always saying I made him nervous and threw him off a bit. I knew the real reason was because he didn't want me to see how much like our father he played, how aggressive he got when he needed to. I actually loved that about my brother—the fact that he didn't take shit lying down and fought for what he wanted.

> **Me: Opening day? Wow! I would love to.**
>
> **Adam: Can I pick you up at 5?**
>
> **Me: It's a date.**

"My?" Brayden lightly tapped his fingertips on my bedroom door.

"Yeah?" I rolled over as he started to enter my

room.

He was still in his sweats from practice. "How'd the date go?"

I propped myself up on my elbow. "It was really nice. I'm going to see him again tomorrow night."

"I'm glad it went well. He better treat you right!" Brayden growled a little, pointing his finger at me.

"Promise. He's one of the good ones. You have a big day tomorrow. Get some sleep."

He nodded. "I'm excited. Sleep well, sis."

"You too, bro."

TWELVE

Myla

Walking into the Otters' arena was thrilling; it had been far too long since I had been to a game. The smell of the ice, the cool air, the bustling of fans all decked out in Otters apparel—it was all freaking amazing.

I started to lead the way, then realized I didn't exactly know where I was going. "Wait, where are our seats?" I glanced around, soaking in the life force of the fans' excitement.

Adam looked down, checking the row and seat numbers on the tickets gripped in his hand. "We're all the way down in front next to the penalty box."

Freaking perfect.

The seats were incredible, but their location meant there was no way Brayden was not going to see me. Knowing my brother, he was going to spend at least a little bit of time in trouble.

We took our seats, chomping on popcorn. "You know; this is my first hockey game." Adam blushed a little as he confessed his naiveté when it came to my favorite sport of all time.

"Don't worry, babe. I can explain the rules to you."

I leapt to my feet as the opposing team started to skate out onto the ice, booing and screaming with the rest of the Otters' fandom. Grabbing Adam's hand, I pulled him up next to me. "You have to yell really loud when they announce Brayden Cox, okay? He's number sixty-eight."

He gave me a sideways glance. "Isn't Cox your last name?"

My face got hot as I bit my lower lip. "Yes. My brother is one of the players."

"No shit. Why didn't you tell me?"

I shrugged. "I wanted you to like me for me, not for who my brother is or who my dad was."

Adam took a sip from his mixed drink, which I could barely smell without almost losing my lunch—Jäger mixed with anything was just so disgusting to me. I couldn't understand how anyone could enjoy a licorice-flavored alcohol. "I get it. I do like you and I don't really know anything about hockey, so it is kind of nice to have an expert here with me."

"Let's just hope for a barn burner!" I yelled, clapping when I saw my brother's number coming onto the ice. "Yay! Brayden!" I screamed with my hands cupped around my mouth, jumping up and down.

Adam leaned closer to my ear. "What's a barn

burner?"

"Oh, honey, you have a lot to learn."

Gavin

I smacked Crosby on the pads as I started to get fired up for the opening game. I could see the flames kindling in my teammates' eyes as we chanted in the locker room. I could feel that the season was going to ours; it had to be. We were coming off a losing streak from the last few seasons and it was high time we started kicking ass and taking names.

My father walked in with his perfectly pressed suit and ridiculous otter-print tie that he thought was the fucking tits. "Are you guys ready?" he bellowed.

Everyone howled back with cheerful grunts and yells.

"What are you going to do with the puck?" His face resembled an overly ripened tomato as he waved his clipboard in the air.

We all responded, "Put it in the net!"

"What's that?" I screamed back at my guys.

"Put it in the fucking net!" they all hollered back to me.

"Let's give them hell, boys!" I shouted, raising my stick in the air.

With that we were all rushing out of the locker room and onto the ice. I followed our goalie out. "Keep that glove up, Crosby, and we just might win this."

He chuckled at me through his fishbowl. "You got it, Cap. Raise hell!"

Our opponents were just as revved up as we were. It was definitely going to be a game to go down in the record books—I could feel it deep in my bones.

My blood pumped hard through my veins as Cox passed to me and I heard the puck hit the bottom of the crossbar before shooting right down into the net.

The siren blared as the announcer cheered. "And that's a beautiful bar down from your captain Gavin Hayes and Brayden Cox with the assist."

I skated by my teammates as they started jumping up from the bench, erupting into a full-blown celebration. Cox came up on my left. "Nice shooting, Hayes."

It was the first time we were actually happy to be on the same ice. "Couldn't have done it without you, man."

Right then, an enforcer from the other team got up in Brayden's face. "Oh look, we found ourselves a little pigeon bitch." He cooed like a fucking moron.

"You can go fuck yourself, Belsky!" I yelled as I fist-bumped another one of my players.

The enforcer shoved Hayes' shoulder. "Letting Daddy protect you, little pigeon?"

Before I could stop him, Cox's gloves were off and he had the douchebag's jersey up over his head as he pummeled the poor shmuck's face.

The referee was quick to respond and the fight was over before Belsky could even get a punch in on Cox. "Way to give them a power play. Next time let them chirp all they want and take out your aggression on the ice, not his face."

I turned to see Belsky spitting blood and a few chiclets onto the ice. "Maybe you should be careful who you shit talk to." I chuckled while skating over to the bench to take a much-needed break.

Brayden

Fuming was putting it mildly—my blood was boiling. All I wanted to do was finish kicking that jerk's ass. I knew Coach was going to give me tons of shit for knocking a guy's teeth out within the first five minutes of the game, but Belsky had it coming. I was not some damn pigeon and I sure as shit was going to prove that.

Someone slamming their fist onto the glass of the

penalty box broke me from my rage-filled haze. I turned to lock eyes with my little sister as she screamed at me.

"Brayden, what the ever-loving fuck was that? Don't let them get under your skin."

I watched as the seconds ticked by on my penalty time. "What in God's name are you fucking doing here?"

As if things weren't already bad enough, now I had to be worried that Myla was going to be pissed at me, too. I didn't really know why it bothered me so much for her to see me act like that; it was no different than what our old man had done to fight his way to the top.

"Adam brought me. Don't be mad." She gave me her damn puppy-dog face that melted my heart.

"We'll talk about this later." My time ended and I burst out onto the ice to seek my revenge. I knew I couldn't punch the guy again, but that didn't mean I couldn't make his time in the rink a living hell in other ways.

After my minute on the ice, I was sitting on the bench next to Gavin. "Sorry, man." I knew I needed to say something before my ass got completely chewed out.

He tapped his stick to mine. "Shit happens, dude. You seemed to have a pretty rough time in the box. Who was that chick?"

I sucked in a sharp breath through my teeth. "Myla's here with some dude I haven't met yet. I fucking hate when she is at my games, especially when I lose my temper like that."

Gavin

Right when Cox said his sister was there, the flame that had been lit in my belly detonated into a full-fledged wildfire consuming every inch of my body.

"Coach! Put me in." My dad nodded, whistled for a change, and I was back out on the ice.

Immediately, I was being slammed hard right in front of the woman I was trying to impress. There was a way her eyes awakened as I got checked into the boards that drew me in. Myla jumped to her feet, smacking her petite hands onto the glass, yelling at my attacker through red lipstick and bright white teeth, a glimmer of an excited smile dancing across her face, colliding with her rage. I knew in that instant that I needed to get to know her spirit, feel that fire, dive into that passion—and I didn't even know anything about her other than the fact that she was my teammate's sister and her name was Myla. I checked out her date: same fucking dude that had been with her the night before, probably her boyfriend, but he was only a speed bump. In one second my heart was kick-started again, and I needed to win that game just for her.

I got the puck and charged the net. I was in a

complete zone. Hearing the alarm sound for my second goal of the game was electrifying; there was not going to be any stopping me that night.

"Keep the foot on the gas, boys! The foot on the gas!" I yelled during a change.

"Aye, Cap!" Paddock called back to me as he sped off.

I counted down my sixty seconds, watching for my next turn. It was the longest minute of my freaking life.

Crosby gloved the puck with another awesome save for the evening. I was stoked at how on the ball all my teammates were. It was sad to admit, but Cox's little display in the beginning really got everyone fired up. Sometimes you just have to kick someone's ass to get the testosterone flowing in the rest of the guys.

I jumped over the wall and bee-lined it for a faceoff. I loved the shit talking; it was a great part of the game for me.

The ref held the puck in the air.

"Keep your head up, Hayes."

Fischer had been traded the season before I started playing for the Otters and I knew he was still bitter about it. "You're the last person I'm scared of, you ugly cunt waffle."

"You fucking want to go?" Fischer was ready to throw down right there, but I had my eye on another prize.

The ref blew his whistle and I charged, throwing my shoulder right into his breadbasket, getting the puck over to Cox. Even as a young player, he was definitely our fastest puck handler, and I needed him to keep his head in the game. It was like he could read my mind as we drove the puck down deep into enemy territory.

"And that's a hat trick for Hayes!" My first freaking hat trick ever and it was on opening day. I couldn't even believe my ears as the crowd exploded into hysteria and threw their hats onto the ice.

THIRTEEN

Myla

"Can you believe it? A fucking hat trick and a shutout for their first game of the season—I mean this is like history in the making." I was skipping to Adam's car, swinging our interlocked hands as excitement coursed through my body.

"I know nothing about hockey, but that was pretty incredible." Adam flashed his toothy grin at me before opening my door and helping me into the passenger's seat.

I whipped my phone out to text Brayden.

> **Me: Holy shit, bro!**
>
> **Brayden: Fuck! I know! I'm glad you were there to experience that**
>
> **Me: Me too. Maybe I am the Otters' lucky charm.**
>
> **Brayden: If that's the case, you better be ready to pack your bags and go on the road with us**

Me: I think Simon would kill me

Brayden: Come out with us tonight

Me: I'll see if Adam wants to

"Want to grab a late night snack? I can't call stale popcorn and a few drinks a proper dinner." He put his hand on my knee. "Or I can think of some other fun things we could do."

With the car still in park, Adam leaned over to start kissing my neck, sliding his hand up my thigh. "I think it's best if you just take me home."

"Come on, baby. I can tell you're into me," he hissed in my ear, shifting in his seat to get better access to me.

"Adam, I don't think this is a good idea."

He bit my neck a little. "Oh, come on. You're all pumped up from the win...let's use that energy to our advantage."

With my phone still in my hand, I clicked to call my brother.

Please pick up.

I saw that the call connected. "Adam, I said no!" I made sure my voice was loud enough that my brother would be able to hear me through the phone.

"Why are you being such a prude? I know there's a wild side under that bookworm exterior of yours just dying to be let out of her cage."

Brayden

I heard Myla yell, "I said just take me home, Adam."

"Fuck!" I growled, stripping down to my base layer as fast as humanly possible.

Gavin looked over at me while pulling his jersey up over his head. "Cox, you good?"

Why the fuck is he being nice to me all of a sudden?

"It's Myla. I think she's getting messed with by that guy."

Gavin started to strip down in rapid fire, too. "What the fuck are we still doing here then?" We both yanked on sweats and sprinted out of the locker room with our hockey sticks in hand. "They're probably in the parking garage. There is a VIP section for those seats they were in, this way."

Flying down the stairs of the parking garage, my mind was on one thing: killing that dude before he took advantage of my sister.

We found the only parked car in the VIP section. *Of course he would drive a Maserati GranTurismo, my damn dream car.*

I started banging on the fogged up window, trying to yank open the locked door. I heard Myla scream from inside. "Bray! Help!"

"Shut the fuck up, bitch!" A slap rang out and I rammed the knob of my stick into the window, glass shattering everywhere. Gavin dove into the driver's seat, pulling Adam out by his throat.

"Who the fuck are you calling a bitch?" Gavin and I yanked the dude out, letting the broken glass scrape against his sleeves, ripping the shirt and letting blood run free.

Myla jumped out of the car, running over next to me as Gavin and I kicked the ever-loving shit out of the dude's ribs.

She had tears streaming down her face, mascara running everywhere. "Guys! That's enough. Don't fucking kill him!"

"Think you're going to rape my little sister, punk-ass bitch?" My adrenaline was pumping as Myla's hand wrapped around my wrist.

"Bray! Gavin! He's not worth it."

Red and blue flashing lights lit up the parking garage as two officers started rushing toward us.

"Officers! Thank God!" Myla screamed. "This man was trying to rape me."

The douche was moaning like a little bitch, rolling around on the ground as he held his broken ribs. He spit on the ground, letting blood spray everywhere. "Officers," he pleaded. "I was just having a moment with my girl when these two guys jumped me."

Myla walked over to him, stomping right down onto his stomach. "You piece of shit!"

One of the cops grabbed her, putting her hands behind her back. "That's assault, missy."

"He was trying to rape me! My brother and Gavin rescued me."

The second officer started to help the guy to his feet while looking over at Gavin and me as both of us seethed. "Is that true?"

I threw my hands into the air. "Don't you think I would much rather be in the showers or headed to the bar to celebrate with my team?"

The cop holding Myla squinted at us. "Holy fuck! No way! You're Cox and Hayes. Man, we listened to the game on the radio tonight. You two killed it! Nice job on that hat trick."

Thank God for fans in uniform.

Gavin smiled at them. "My buddy Sean Whistler can vouch for me, man. We were just protecting the lady."

The officer let go of Myla. "Would you like to make a statement?"

She shook her head. "No, I think Adam got what was coming to him."

Adam. What a punk-ass name.

"I would like to press charges," Adam said, coughing a little as he leaned on the hood of the cop car.

Both of the officers started laughing. "Yeah, we don't think so, tiger."

He got all pissy. "You'll all be hearing from my lawyer."

I grabbed Myla, pulling her into my arms as she started to sob again.

"You scum-sucking jerkoff, fucking bring it." I spit on the ground at his feet. "I ain't scared of you or your lawyers, and if you come near my sister again, a few broken ribs will be the least of your worries."

"Aren't you going to do anything?" Adam threw his hands up, waving at the cops. "He just threatened me."

The older of the two cops slapped him on the shoulder. "I heard a man protecting a woman after she was attacked. I would suggest you get in your car and leave now before this young lady changes her mind and you get booked for attempted rape."

"This is fucking unbelievable. Fucking cunt," Adam hissed as he walked past us.

"What did you just call her?" Gavin wound up and knocked him square in the jaw.

The officers both looked at each other, shrugging.

"I think I told you to leave, sir."

Adam got in his car, revving the engine loudly before speeding away.

"Perfect." One of officers smiled. "Now we can rope him for reckless driving. You all get home safe tonight."

They jumped into their car and sped away, siren blaring, chasing Adam down.

"Well, he had that one coming to him. What an idiot." Gavin picked up our sticks and handed me mine.

"Thanks, man." I slapped him on the shoulder.

"Hey, we take care of our own, right?"

Myla rushed over to Gavin, kissing him on the cheek. "This really means a lot to me."

Gavin gave her a quick hug. "I could use a drink. What about you?"

"She's only twenty, man. I should probably take her home anyway."

Myla looked from Gavin to me. "No, we have a win to celebrate. Fuck Adam. I am not going to let him ruin this for us."

"Well, all right then. We're about to take you where many puck bunnies have been before." Gavin gave her a little wink as he started to lead the way back up to the locker room.

"What?" Myla shot me a confused look.

I chuckled at her while wiping the smudged makeup out from under her eye. Even after crying her eyes out, she looked gorgeous. I was starting to realize that my sister was not a little girl anymore and it was killing me. "Well, we can't have you going out all dolled up with us having swamp ass, now can we? We haven't even showered yet."

FOURTEEN

Gavin

We were breaking the rules, but if Myla wanted to stay with Brayden and me, she sure as shit was not going to leave our sides for the rest of the night. Hearing that douchenozzle slap her had been more aggravating than any other moment in my entire life.

I peeked into the locker room. "Anyone in here?" I called in.

Without thinking, I grabbed Myla's hand to lead her into the locker room. "Everyone must have just left."

I took my cell out of my gym bag and saw dozens of missed calls and texts from the players. Scrolling through, I saw that they had made their way to a bar just down the street from the arena.

Brayden showed Myla around. "A lot has changed since Dad was a player." She gazed around, turning up her nose a bit. "Smells about the same though. Boy does hockey gear fucking reek to high heaven."

"We play hard. It's the smell of men and victory." I flashed her a quick smile, clutching my change of clothes and a towel.

Brayden was right behind me, giving his sister a reassuring tap on the shoulder. "We'll be quick. You can use the mirror over there to fix your makeup if you want."

She rolled her eyes. "That means I need to fix my face, doesn't it?"

I laughed as Brayden ate his words, turning on the water to as hot as it could go. Usually after an intense game, I iced down my sore muscles and then relaxed with a nice hot shower, but I could already feel my aches and bruises attacking my body; I was going to pay for it later for sure.

We all made quick work of getting in and out. We were going to get the third degree at the bar, but I didn't give a shit.

Walking into the packed joint, everyone started to cheer.

"Finally!" Crosby handed Brayden and me longnecks. "We were starting to think you two ditched us."

Brayden clinked his bottle with Crosby's. "Nah man. Just had to take care of something really quick."

"We're here now and that's what matters." I chugged half the bottle on the spot.

Out of the corner of my eye, I saw Myla take a seat

in a corner booth by herself. Bringing her a water, I took a seat next to her.

"You don't have to worry about me. Go party with your guys."

I waved my hand at the rowdy crowd. "They're all about three sheets to the wind by now. Us just being here is enough. How're you holding up?"

She started to pull apart a tiny bar napkin. "I think I am in shock. It all feels like a movie I watched, not something I lived."

The red mark on her cheek was starting to fade a little. "Does it hurt? Should I get you some ice?"

She cocked her head to one side. "Hayes, aren't you supposed to be some asshat that treats women like pieces of meat?"

I feigned a smile. "Rumors get started with a kernel of truth, I guess." Taking a sip from my Bud Light to fill a little of the awkward silence, I tried to think of something clever to follow up with. "I mean, I was engaged. It's not like I am a total dick to all women."

Myla shrugged. "You seem pretty all right in my book, Hayes."

"Did you enjoy the gong show at least?"

It was the first time all night she actually smiled. "It was an incredible game. I'm really glad I got to see it."

"As am I." I worked my jaw, trying to keep the conversation flowing. "So, where do you live exactly?"

She swallowed the ice cube she had been rolling around in her mouth. "East Flushing, close to Kissena Park."

"Oh well la di da," I teased.

"Shut up." She playfully shoved my arm. "You probably live in some fancy rent-controlled apartment in one of the buildings your family owns."

"Actually, I am moving into my own place, out from under my dad's thumb, this weekend. You should come by and check it out." A few girls walked in through the door, half of whom I had banged at one time or another over the last few years. "Shit," I muttered as two of them started to waggle their way over to me.

"Hey, Hayes, you were awesome tonight." Rita was one of the sluttiest puck bunnies I had ever seen; she followed our players around like a junkie in search of her next fix.

I put my arm around Myla's shoulders. "Please, just go with this," I whispered to her before diverting my glare to Rita and Jinny. "Thanks. Have you met Myla?" I pulled Myla into my side a little and she followed my lead perfectly.

"Sweetie, who are your friends?" She leaned her elbow on the table, giving them the evil eye.

"Didn't think you were wifed up, Hayes," Jinny hissed before sucking on her front teeth. She was fucking gross—I couldn't believe my dick ever got up for that slut.

I leaned in, grabbing Myla by the back of the head and kissing her hard. *That should do the trick.*

Myla

Is Gavin Hayes really kissing me right now?

I grabbed his rock hard bicep and gave the best show I could. It wasn't rocket science to figure out he was trying to get the two women off of his dick for the night.

In a huff the two wandered up to the bar, fawning over a few of the other players.

"Thanks," Gavin said breathily, pulling his lips away from mine.

I batted my eyelashes dramatically. "Oh, sweetheart, you know you can kiss me whenever you want to." I elbowed him in the ribs and he winced. "You okay?"

He nodded. "Yeah, just got checked pretty good tonight."

I bit my lip; I knew the moment he was talking about, and it had been a thrilling part of the game for me. "I was ready to rip Belsky's throat out at that point. Messing with my boys like that—what fucking nerve!"

"Your boys, huh?" He downed the rest of his beer.

"Well, I have been pretty invested in the Otters for as long as I can remember, so yes, you guys are mine. I have claimed you."

He got up from the booth, reaching out his hand to me. "Come on, let's celebrate this awesome win."

I took Gavin's hand, glancing over to see my brother's face fill with rage. "Give me a second." Gavin nodded and went to hang out with a cluster of players at the far end of the bar.

"How's it going, bro?"

He sucked in through his front teeth. "He's charming, but he'll end up showing his true colors eventually, My."

Brayden was already a few beers deep; I could tell it was getting to the point where I needed to get him home. "He's just being friendly."

Brayden slammed his empty beer bottle down onto the bar top. "Scotch neat," he yelled before turning back to me. "I saw him kiss you. I wasn't born fucking yesterday."

"Bray, he was trying to get those chicks to leave him alone, and I was just helping. It's not like I am in the bathroom blowing him right now."

Brayden looked like he was about to blow chunks at the thought. "Fuck, Myla. Where the hell did you learn to talk like that?"

I flipped my hair, giving my brother a coy smile. "I read a lot. I'm not as naïve as you think I am."

He grabbed my hand. "I just don't want to see you

get hurt, and he's my captain for Christ's sake. I don't want to have to hate him for any other reason than him being a pompous twat from time to time."

I signaled to the bartender right before she was about to pour Brayden's drink. "Hold off on that one. We're going to head home."

Brayden sighed, pulling out his wallet. "Won't even let me have a good time with my friends, making out with my damn captain—now I know why I don't bring you around." He gave me a quick wink, leaning in to whisper, "Kidding, sis. You're right, it's definitely time for me to ice down my knee and call it a night."

Gavin came up behind us. "Leaving so soon?" He hooked his arm around my brother's neck. "You're taking my beard away."

Brayden laughed. "She's making me. It's all her fault."

Gavin snuck a napkin into my hand. "Get home safely, you two. Cox, I'll see you in the barn tomorrow."

FIFTEEN

Myla

"Wait. Hold on! Let me get this straight." Simon sipped on his Cosmo with his pinky high in the air. "Adam tried to assault you, Gavin and your brother beat him up, you kissed Gavin Hayes and then he gave you his number on a bar napkin, but you haven't even put it into your phone yet?"

I stared down at the napkin with Gavin's scribbled number on it. "That's the basic gist of the evening's events. Crazy right?"

"I just cannot believe you waited three whole days to tell me this and you haven't even contacted that hunky hockey player yet. He's obviously into you! And I am just so shocked at how Adam behaved. I never pegged him for a rapist."

I took a bite of my tuna sashimi before responding. "I think the Unabomber's friends said the same thing about that crackpot."

Simon chuckled. "You're probably right. I just feel so awful because I set you two up."

"There was no way for you to know. He was very charming, to say the least—well, in the beginning that is."

Simon grabbed my phone and the napkin from my hand. "We're texting Gavin. They're traveling home today, right?"

"They should be home by now. They had another win last night, and they play the Sharks here tomorrow." I wanted to fight Simon for my phone, but a small part of me was excited that he was going to text Gavin. I was just so freaking nervous that he had been drunk at the bar and didn't really want me to have his number.

"Perfect excuse to send him a little congratulations text then."

Simon typed away on my phone, reading the text out loud to me. "Hey Gavin, sorry for my delay, it's been a crazy couple of days. Great win last night."

I shrugged. "Whatever you think is best."

He beamed, singing, "Simon says! And sent."

Handing me back my phone, he flagged down the server to bring us another boat of sashimi and him another Cosmo.

"Who is going to eat all of that?" I glared down at our still half-full first boat.

With a sly grin on his face, he narrowed his eyes. "Trust me, we'll be needing it."

My phone buzzed across the table as a couple texts came through.

Gavin: Hey, you! I've been thinking of you.

Gavin: I just walked in the door to my new place with nothing but a bed in it, trying to figure out what to have for dinner.

Gavin: What are you up to?

I shrieked a little as my face and ears got warm. "He texted back."

Simon leaned back in his chair, a triumphant look plastered on his face. "Invite him to eat some of our sushi."

"Simon, you're one sneaky little queen, aren't you?" I started typing away in response to Gavin.

Me: Just ordered way more sushi than I know what to do with. Join us?

Gavin: Us? And where?

Me: My boss, Simon Abrams, and I will drop a pin and send it to you.

Gavin: Simon? No shit. He's hilarious. I'll swing by for sure.

Gavin

I changed my shirt three times.

Why the fuck am I this nervous?

I hopped in a cab and was at a hole-in-the-wall Japanese place within thirty minutes of Myla texting me.

Walking in, I saw Simon waving at me from a booth in the back of the tiny restaurant.

"Hey, guys." I slid in next to Myla. "Thanks for the invite. I don't even have plates at my new place yet. You saved me from eating pizza on the floor."

"Glad you could make it." Myla could barely even look at me.

Guess we're both nervous—that's a good sign.

"How was the game last night?" Simon asked before downing the last of his fruity cocktail.

"We're playing better than we have in years. Looks like all those sessions with you teaching us skating techniques are paying off for sure." The server came over and I ordered green tea.

Myla gave me a sideways look, raising an eyebrow at me. "Who are you?" she teased.

"What? I don't drink every day during the season. I need to stay on my A game and hangovers definitely put a damper on that."

Simon reached into his pocket, checking his phone. "Well, look at the time. I have to be up *so* early for a private session." He pulled some money out of his wallet. "I need to head out. Kisses."

He blew kisses at Myla, who was pointing at him with a narrowed glare. "I know what you're doing, sir.

You sly motherfucker."

Simon gasped. "Me? No! You know how easily I lose track of time."

He was gone in a flash. "Did we just get set up?" I threw a piece of eel into my mouth.

Myla pursed her lips. "I cannot believe him sometimes. I'm sorry."

I put my hand on her shoulder. "Honestly, I came here for you. I've been thinking about you a lot over the last few days. How're you holding up?"

She looked down at her plate, mixing more wasabi into her soy sauce with a chopstick. "I've been okay. Seven has been helping keep me busy."

"Seven?"

She pulled out her phone, giddy to show me pictures. "She's a husky puppy. Brayden got her for me not too long ago so I wouldn't be lonely when you guys were traveling."

I flipped through the dozens of pictures Myla had. "She's adorable."

We spent the next few hours engrossed in conversation, ranging from hockey to our childhoods to Myla's father, all the way back to lighthearted comedies and standup we both enjoyed.

I snorted as Myla laughed uncontrollably. "*Cable Guy* is by far my favorite Jim Carrey movie of all time."

"The password is nipple," I whispered in her ear,

trying to keep a straight face.

She whipped her head around, not missing a beat. "I can't say that to my mother!" Myla pulled off the flabbergasted tone and facial expression flawlessly.

"It's just skin, Steven," I replied, then we were both in stitches.

Myla's phone started ringing. "It's Brayden, I better take this."

She answered quickly.

"Hey, Bray...Yeah, I fed her...She's fine in her crate until I get home...I'm still eating with Simon. I'll be home soon...Love you, too."

I couldn't quite put my finger on why it bothered me so much that Myla lied to Brayden about being with me. It was completely understandable—I wouldn't want my little sister on a kind-of date with a douchebag like me.

She grabbed my hand, sending electricity through my body. "Sorry, I just know Bray would kill me for being here with you."

I chewed on the side of my cheek. "I get it. I'd be protective too if I had a sister as pretty and sweet as you are."

The blush that dusted her cheeks was adorable. "You think I'm pretty?"

I stared dead into her eyes. "No." I paused, waiting for her to respond, but she just looked down at our hands, releasing mine. I pulled her chin to make her look at me with her steely blue eyes. "I think you're incredible. Beautiful doesn't even graze the surface of what you are."

She leaned in and gave me a simple, slow kiss. "Thank you."

"For being honest? You're very welcome, love."

She looked at the time on her phone. "I really should be heading home."

I wanted to grab her and never let her go. I had never been that drawn to another person in my life, not even my ex-fiancée, and it scared the shit out of me.

She started to grab money out of her purse and I put my hand on hers, stopping her. "What do you think you're doing young lady?"

She looked up at me, confused. "Paying the bill? I did order all this without you."

I kissed her cheek. "And I am so glad you did, but I will not let you pay for this."

"I have money, Gavin. I don't need you to."

I shook my head at her. "I know you're a strong, independent woman, *and* I want to take care of you, so please, just let me."

SIXTEEN

Myla

The next few days went by with Gavin and I texting nonstop. He was slowly becoming a complete addiction. Walking with Seven back to our house from a long jaunt around Kissena Park, I pulled out my phone to see Gavin's name scrolling across my screen. *Insta-butterflies.*

> Gavin: Are you going to come to the game tonight?
>
> Me: I have a private session, so I can't.
>
> Gavin: When can I see you again?
>
> Me: Tomorrow night?
>
> Gavin: I literally will be counting down the seconds.

Putting my coat on the rack by the front door, I turned right into Brayden.

"Hey, watch where you're going."

I had the biggest shit-eating grin on my face,

rereading Gavin's last text over and over. "What?" I looked up at my brother, who had both hands on his hips and was tapping his foot.

"Well, what do we have here? Someone is all lit up like a damn Christmas tree for some reason."

I had to play it off fast. "You know how silly Simon can be with his stupid *Simon Says* bull." I rolled my eyes, shoving my phone back into my pocket.

Me: Do you want me to come over?

Gavin: How many ways do I have to say it, Myla? Of course I do. I wouldn't have invited you yesterday if I didn't.

Me: Ok. I'll leave as soon as Bray is asleep.

Gavin: Your brother still doesn't know you're hanging out with me?

Me: Does it make a difference?

Gavin: Right now? Not in the slightest. We'll talk about that later. Just get your sexy ass to my place now.

Me: All right. He should pass out in thirty minutes or so. Whiskey acts quickly on him.

It was the longest fucking thirty minutes of my

damn life. Finally, Brayden trudged up the stairs and turned off the hallway light.

"Goodnight, My," he called through the door.

"Sleep well." I turned out my light as I heard him shuffle his way to his room.

Only a few more minutes left.

Jumping out of bed, I flipped the light back on, making sure to cover Seven's crate with a blanket after sneaking a huge rawhide in to keep her occupied. She was doing better in there the past couple of nights and I could only hope she wouldn't start barking or crying while I was gone. I requested an Uber and started checking myself out in the mirror for one last look.

Lacy black bra and panties—check.

Showstopper red pumps that made my thighs and ass look perfect—check.

The little black number Simon told me I should never take off—check.

A change of clothes, toothbrush, and makeup for the morning—check.

I didn't even know if I was going to be spending the night, but I needed to be prepared just in case.

Holy hell. I am about to fuck Gavin Hayes.

Is this real life?

Brayden is going to kill me.

The driver messaged me that he was downstairs. *Show time.* I was a bundle of nerves riding in the backseat of the Honda Civic. The young driver tried to make small talk, but I could barely pay attention to him; the anticipation was just too much.

Me: I'm downstairs.

Gavin: The doorman knows you're coming. He'll let you in and swipe you into the elevator.

With shaking knees, I stood in the elevator as I was whisked up to the penthouse Gavin had just moved into.

I took a few deep breaths outside the double doors to PH2 before knocking. The overwhelming feeling of butterflies crashing around in my gut was about to make me hurl. The door flew open and Gavin was wrapping me in his arms before I could even register what was happening.

"Here it is, home sweet home."

There was nothing in his apartment other than a mattress on the far side of the living room with a TV and an Xbox next to it.

"Charming." I nudged him with an elbow before leaning down to set my bag against the wall.

"Hey now, brat. The movers are coming in the morning. Planning on staying a while?" Gavin asked while running a gentle hand over my ass.

I giggled nervously, spinning on my heels. "A girl needs to be prepared, my dear."

Gavin hooked his arm around my waist. "I like that."

He kissed my cheek, breathing softly into my ear. "I'm really glad you're here."

I laced my fingers with his. "So am I, babe."

He growled a little. "I like the way *babe* sounds rolling off your lips. Want a tour?" He took me by the hand, showing me the large open space. "We have the kitchen, dining room, living room." He pointed all around. "Then down the hall I have two bedrooms and bathrooms. Nothing in them yet, as you can see."

"I like it." I walked over to the sliding door that led out to a humongous balcony. The cold night air swirled around me as I took in the breathtaking view of the most amazing city in the world.

Joining me out on the balcony, Gavin grabbed me. "I'm hungry," he whispered.

"For what?" I questioned as he kissed my neck.

"For you." Picking me up into his arms, Gavin carried me over to the bed.

"You're not going to be needing these." He pulled my heels off, throwing them across the room. The rawness in his kisses and touch was inebriating.

"We don't have to do anything but lie here all night and watch stupid shit on Netflix."

"I didn't get all dressed up to actually Netflix and chill, Gavin." I grabbed the back of his neck, crushing our lips together. He wasn't the only one that was hungry.

A low growl came from the back of his throat. "I

like that." He gradually unzipped my dress. "Next time just wear yoga pants and a shirt. Be comfortable around me. You're gorgeous on your own—you don't need to get dolled up to turn me on."

My entire body was trembling as I tried to unbutton his dress shirt. I could feel the heat radiating from my cheeks as I fumbled with the buttons.

Get a grip, woman. He's totally into you.

"Don't worry, Myla, I got this. All I want is for you to relax and let me do everything."

His lips brushed against mine as his fingertips trailed up my inner thigh, all the way to my soaking panties. Tenderly, he started to rub the lace.

"Oh, fuck. Gavin." The words came out so softly I could barely hear them myself, but his breath hitched as his nails dug into my delicate flesh a bit.

"Ugh, babe, I love hearing you say my name." He pulled my dress up over my head, taking a moment to let his eyes travel up and down my body. "You're fucking perfect."

All I could think about were my surgery scars and lack of toned muscle; I had no idea what on God's green earth he could think was fucking perfect about that.

"I'm not," I whispered as he kissed down my shoulder.

His hot breath traveled over my skin. "Yes, Myla, you're incredible, and sexy, and perfect. One day, I will make you see it."

He quickly undressed while we made out like two horny high schoolers on the way to prom.

"I'm going to have to take my time with you," he whispered, kissing down my chest, nipping at my breasts.

"I don't want you to hold back."

I could feel his muscles tense. "There's a beast in me and once I let it out, I can't control it."

I licked his ear slowly. "Good. Take me, Gavin. I'm yours."

"Be careful what you wish for little girl." His voice was gravely as he bit down on my shoulder, sending chills down my spine.

He flipped me over onto my stomach, pulling my ass up a bit. "Fucking perfection." His hands gripped my bare ass as he sucked in a sharp breath. He leaned down, kissing from the top of my spine all the way down my back. "Give me one second."

I heard a condom wrapper rip open. I rolled over to put my hand on his.

"Who told you to move, little one?" His eyes narrowed as I bit my lip.

"I want to feel all of you. I'm on the pill."

He threw the condom to the floor. "I just got checked out, I'm clean, but...are you sure?" It was nice that he wanted to be absolutely certain I wasn't just trying to give him what I thought he wanted. "I don't want to make you uncomfortable, babe."

"Then listen to me," I teased before getting back into the position he had put me in.

Gavin rubbed my swelling clit with his thumb. "You're so wet already, baby."

I moaned as he gently drove the head of his dick into me, grabbing my hands and holding my wrists together behind my back. "Holy hell, Myla. You're so tight."

Slowly he started to thrust in and out, deeper into me each time. I started to grind my hips back into his. He smacked my ass. "I told you I was going to do everything. Now just be still like a good girl, baby."

His fingers laced into my hair, pulling my head back a bit as his teeth sunk into my neck.

"Gavin." I breathed deeply as my climax started to build quickly. "You're going to make me come."

"Good." He growled in my ear. "I want you to come for me first."

My body started to shake and tense as the most euphoric orgasm of my life crashed around me. "Holy fuck." I panted, my body covered in sweat. "That was my first non-battery-induced orgasm."

"There's a first time for everything, babe. I'm glad I was able to give it to you."

Gavin rolled me over onto my back, climbing on top of me. "My turn." His lips pulled at the corners for the sexiest smirk I had ever seen on him.

I let my thumb travel over his lips. "That smile, I've never seen it before."

He kissed me quickly before pounding hard and deep into my pussy. "It's because you bring out a different side of me."

His pace quickened, and I could feel his dick starting to twitch deep inside me, causing another climax to come on within seconds. His breath hitched as his knees trembled and he bit down hard on my shoulder.

"You're fucking incredible." He panted, rolling off of me.

I curled up into his arm as he stroked my hair. "So are you."

SEVENTEEN

Gavin

Waking up with Myla sleeping naked in my bed was the most amazing thing I could have ever imagined. Kissing her cheek, I whispered into her ear, "I'm going to hop in the shower, love."

She moaned, rolling away from me and pulling a pillow over her head.

Letting the hot water get the perfect temperature, I climbed in to let my sore muscles relax. It was true what they said: if you want to win a game, you have to be beat up and bruised by the end of it—otherwise you're not fighting hard enough for it.

"Gavin?" Myla peaked her head into the bathroom, wrapped in my sheet.

"Hey babe. Want to jump in?"

She scampered over to the shower door, dropping the sheet at her feet. "It's fucking freezing in your place."

"Yes, but it's nice and warm in here."

I pulled her in close, rubbing my hands over the goose bumps on her arms. She sweetly kissed my bicep as her fingertips rolled down my abs and over my dick. Before I could make any moves, she was down on her knees with my cock in her mouth. I threw my hand against the wall as my knees started buckling under me. "Holy fuck, babe. If this is how you say good morning, I will make you a key today."

She looked up at me, smiling with her mouth full—it was the sexiest look I had ever seen in my life.

"Get up," I snarled, pulling her up by her arm and throwing her against the cold tile. Sinking my teeth into her chest, I could feel her heart start racing as I shoved two fingers into her dripping cunt.

Kneeling in front of her, I let my tongue finally taste what I had been craving since the first moment I had laid eyes on her. Her tangy sweetness consumed me as her body started to shake against me, riding my face as her orgasm took control.

"Holy fucking shit." She was breathing so heavily as her nails dug into my shoulders. I felt her pussy tighten as she moaned, throwing her head back.

Getting back to my feet, I pulled her up into my arms, railing her against the wall until we were both coming together again.

"So, do I really get a key?" Myla teased, rinsing herself off before using my body wash to clean up.

"Babe, you could ask me for anything right now and I would say yes."

Brayden

Pacing around the living room, trying Myla's phone again for the tenth time that morning, I was really starting to get worried.

I front door creaked open. "My? Is that you?"

She tiptoed in with dripping hair, her heels in hand. "Hey, Brayden. Man, you're up early."

I looked down at Seven, who was jumping down from the couch, waging her tail furiously, running to greet Myla. "Your dog started freaking out a couple hours ago. Where have you been? I've been calling you."

She diverted her gaze, kneeling down next to her puppy, who was now licking her face relentlessly. "I went out with some friends last night, and it got late so I crashed there. No big deal."

"No big deal?" I yelled. "What the fuck do you mean *friends?* You have one fucking friend and that's Simon. I know you weren't with him because I already called his gay ass and he was with some dude named Raul all night."

"Fuck, Brayden, get off my ass. I have a damn life outside this house."

141

I threw my hands in the air. "Can you just tell me where you were? I've been worried sick."

"Fine!" She was huffing, on the verge of tears. "I was with a guy and you're going to fucking hate me for this."

Cue the waterworks.

"That shit isn't going to fly, Myla. Just tell me, damn it!"

"I was with Gavin. Are you fucking happy?"

I punched the wall. "Myla, I asked you to stay away from him. Of all the people in the world, you go sneaking off with the captain of my damn team? Is this really happening right now?"

She started to run up the stairs. "Fuck you, Brayden. You don't get to tell me who to love."

Love? Did my sister just confess to me that she is in love with Gavin Hayes? Fuck my life—hell has just frozen over.

I heard her door slam and her lock click.

I flew into the locker room like a bat out of hell and Gavin threw his hands in the air. "Look, man. Let's talk this one out."

He was trying to play nice after fucking my sister all night. *Fuck that.*

"You're a fucking dead man, Hayes. Couldn't keep your dick out of my sister could you?"

I punched him right in the eye.

As he stumbled back, leaning against the wall, he looked at me. "It's different with her, bro. I would never hurt her."

"*Bro*? Did you really just call me bro?" I was ready to deck him again, but Crosby was standing between us. "I know how you treat all your girls, Gavin. You fuck them and leave them. You don't care about anyone but yourself."

Gavin walked over to me, put his hand on my shoulder, and stared me dead in my eyes. "I'm falling for her dude. This isn't like the others. Shit, this isn't even like Marsheila. I love her, Brayden, and I will fight to be with her."

"You're a dead man if you hurt her! Do you fucking hear me?" I could barely control my breathing.

"If I hurt her, I'll quit the team." As serious as a heart attack, Gavin stared into my eyes. "I mean it. You have my word."

We shook hands, but I only did it because I didn't want to get benched for the rest of the season. "I'm going to hold you to that."

EIGHTEEN

Gavin

A few months later

Waking up to texts from Myla was my favorite. Seeing her quirky humor was so freaking perfect to me.

Myla: Morning handsome.

Me: Hey babe. What are you doing up so early?

Myla: Heading into Central Park to get a good run in. With you and Brayden on the road, I have to fill my day off somehow.

Me: True.

Myla: You're never going to believe what just happened! I cannot stop laughing.

Me: What?!

Myla: A chick on the train just answered her phone, "Hello, Hillary Swallows..."

Me: That is classic! I would have spit out my coffee laughing.

Myla: I picked up my head and locked eyes with the chick across from me. We were both trying to fight giggles when she raised an eyebrow and leaned over to say, "I bet she does..."

Me: Fucking amazing!

Myla: Both of us are still giggling like little kids. I like when people are on my juvenile wavelength.

Me: I can't wait to be home to you, baby.

Myla: You'll be back before you know it. Kick some ass tonight. I'll be at Simon's watching the game with him and Raul.

Me: Raul?

Myla: Simon has a new boyfriend. I haven't met him yet, but Simon is pretty enthralled to say the least.

After getting out of bed, I walked down the hall and knocked on Brayden's door.

He opened it, letting me in reluctantly.

"Are we still not okay?" I asked, leaning against the desk as he threw an Otters t-shirt on.

"I don't know, man. I mean she seems to be the happiest she's ever been, so I'm trying to be all right with this."

"Thanks." It was the only thing to say, and it meant a lot to me that Brayden was at least trying. "So, Myla's birthday is the day after our next home game, right?"

Brayden nodded. "What were you thinking?" His shoulders relaxed a little as he sat in an armchair across from me.

"Well, I figured we could get the team together and party in the city. We could do something low key, but I thought it would be nice if she saw that we planned something together."

Brayden stretched. "That would mean a lot to her I am sure, and she does love the city this time of year, says the winter makes it magical or some shit."

I couldn't help but get the biggest shit-eating grin on my face, thinking back to the first night in my apartment with her being so happy on my balcony. "We could do something at my place, then we wouldn't have to worry about too much. I know a kickass bartender that would do it up really awesome for us."

"Sounds like a plan to me, but no banging my sister while I am there. I will lose my shit if that happens."

"Deal." We shook on it and I got to work texting Jordan, Sean, and Simon to enlist their help on making it a night Myla was never going to forget.

"Hi, Mom. How're you?" She always called at the worst times. I was already running behind schedule, rushing to the arena for the game.

"Fine. I was talking to Sherryl and she said her daughter never heard back from you after that date a while back." The disappointment in her voice was pissing me off.

"Did you ever think I might not have wanted to go on the date in the first place? That chick was an aspiring housewife for crying out loud."

"Oh, honey, at least she had the nerve to tell you that honestly. Deep down that's what every woman wants. A good provider and to not have to work—it's the American dream."

"I met someone." She was silent.

"Mom?"

She cleared her throat. "I thought that Cox girl was just going to be a fling."

"Are you kidding? How'd you know about Myla?"

"Honey, you're dating one of your teammates' sisters and she's the daughter of one of the biggest embarrassments your franchise has ever had. People talk, you know."

"This conversation is over, Mom. I have a game to win."

She sighed. "Bring her to dinner Sunday night."

"No."

"Your brother is only in town for that evening and you better be there. Bring the girl or not, up to you, but your butt better be in your seat by six when dinner is ready."

"We'll see."

Myla

"Do I look okay?" I twirled for Gavin in my long-sleeved, deep purple dress.

"Stunning as always. Are you sure you're okay with going?" I could see how nervous he was about having me come to his family's dinner.

"It's your family. They're important to you, so they are important to me. I'm excited to finally meet them."

Gavin leaned back on my bed grabbing the brand new copy of Ryker off my nightstand, thumbing through the middle as I finished putting my makeup on.

"You're important to me. They're an obligation."

I glanced at him. "Well, I'm not going anywhere, so I will have to meet them eventually, right?"

He shrugged then nearly choked laughing.

"What?" I questioned, taking a seat next to him.

"This is like fucking porn. I had no idea you read shit like this."

I tried to grab the book out of his hands as he started to read one of the sex scenes that made me blush.

"'I'm trying... but... Oh... Fuck... right there.' I try to beg him not to stop, but the words won't come out. I blink rapidly as my eyes white spots cloud my vision. Holy mother of everything holy... "Oh my god. Shit! I'm gonna..." the waves of pleasure flow through my body as he continues to lick and suck on my clit, dragging my orgasm out. My eyes roll back into my head over and over again. My breathing quickens and a thin sheen of sweat covers my entire body. I've never felt anything like that in my life. Nothing.' "Holy hell, babe. No wonder you're good at talking dirty." He threw the book down onto the bed, grabbing me. "I can think of a lot more fun things we could do if we blew off dinner with my folks."

I kissed him quickly then jumped to my feet. "We are going and if we don't leave now, we're going to be late."

Mansion was an understatement; the Hayes estate

was sprawling. I knew Gavin's parents both came from money, but I had no idea just how much of it they actually had.

We were greeted at the front door by a guy I could only assume was Gavin's brother.

"Holy shit! You actually came. I bet Dad fifty bucks you were going to be a no-show." Gavin hugged his brother before introducing us.

"Griff, meet Myla."

He wrapped me up in a huge hug. "It's nice to meet you," I said as he was releasing his vice grip.

"The pleasure is all mine." Griffin took both of our coats and put them into the closet just outside the foyer.

"So, Gavin told me you were pretty, but he did not do your beauty justice, to say the least." Griffin slapped Gavin's arm. "Damn, bro, no wonder you're holding on to this one."

Gavin snarled at his brother. "Cool it, Griff. I already don't want to be here—don't make this anymore awkward than it needs to be."

We all took seats around the table after I formally met Gavin's parents, neither of whom seemed to want anything to do with Gavin or me. I had no idea why his mother had insisted we make an appearance at dinner if our company wasn't welcome.

After we had a glass of wine with some cheese and crackers in silence, Gavin's mother finally spoke. "So,

Myla, Gavin tells me you're a figure skating coach. Any promising skaters I should be looking for in the next Olympics?"

I must have been as red as red could be. "No ma'am, not yet at least. My girls have quite a while before they'll even be jumping."

"So, you work with peewees then?"

I nodded, not knowing what else to say. "It's really been amazing."

Griff smiled sweetly at me. "Have you been to any of Gavin's games this season?"

"I was at the first one. It was absolutely amazing, to say the least."

Mr. Hayes grunted from the head of the table. He was definitely a man of few words, maybe no words for that matter. *How does he coach like that?*

Gavin grabbed my hand. "This little lady was our good luck charm for sure that night. Cox and I played even harder knowing she was rooting for us."

"Honey, I'm sorry but I just cannot do this." Mrs. Hayes shoved away from the table. "I mean a *Cox* for crying out loud, and you claim to love her? Do you really think that will suit our family? A peewee figure skating assistant coach to a washed-up has-been? This is just awful."

I started to scoot my chair back. "Maybe I should just leave," I whispered to Gavin. Griff started shaking his head, waving his hand at me to stay in my seat.

Griffin followed his mother into the living room. "I'll take care of her. Dad? Want to join me?"

Mr. Hayes grunted, taking his Scotch glass and going the opposite direction of his wife and youngest son. "This is bullshit."

First words I had ever heard the man say and he was piss drunk, swearing about the shit show that had just ensued because his son had brought me home for dinner.

Gavin angrily erupted from the table. "Myla, I'm sorry but I need a minute."

He rushed out the back door and there I sat, alone in a fancy formal dining room with a roasted Cornish hen in front of me like an idiot.

After a few minutes, I found my way to the backyard.

"Gavin?" I walked out to the back patio where he was pacing.

"Babe, I am so sorry I lost it in there. They just get under my skin."

I grabbed his hand. "Gavin, look at me."

He glanced down, his eyes glassing over as he pulled my coat closed to help me stay warm. "What's up, babe?"

"You cannot light yourself on fire to keep others warm. Just remember that."

Pulling me into him, he sighed. "How did I get so lucky to find you?" He kissed my forehead. "How about we blow this popsicle stand, grab a pizza, and watch Jim Jefferies' new special that just came out?"

Beaming up at the man I loved, I hug him tighter. "That sounds perfect."

After eating my weight in pizza, I curled up under a fluffy blanket in bed with Gavin. Even though the night had started off stressful, there was nothing about these little moments that I would change for the world.

"You know what I don't freaking get?" My inevitable food coma was starting to make me giggly and totally goofy.

Gavin looked down at me, smiling and laughing. "What's that, beautiful?"

I paused Jim Jefferies right as he was telling a story about Oscar Pistorius and how he shot the hottest girl on earth. "Why the fuck is a New York team's mascot an otter? Where the hell did Ollie come from?"

He pulled me closer to him and kissed my cheek. "Do you know how adorable you are?"

"Why is that adorable? I am seriously so confused

by this fact."

"Ollie the Otter was the original owner's daughter's pet. She begged her dad to make him the mascot and she used to bring the damn thing into the owner's box on a leash."

I chewed on the last piece of crust from my paper plate. "That is amazing!" I exclaimed with food still in my mouth. "How the hell did I not know this?"

"Your father and brother apparently slacked on keeping you informed about their team's history, my dear."

"Bray doesn't like talking to me about the team really, or even hockey in general, and my sperm donor can rot in that place for all I care."

"Well, I will talk to you about it, tell you anything you want to know."

"Really?" I cuddled into the crook of his shoulder as a wave of sleepies took over.

"Yes, babe. You're my girl. That means I will tell you anything and everything you want as long as it keeps putting smiles like that on your face."

NINETEEN

Gavin

Everyone was crammed into my apartment with the lights off, hushed. "She'll be coming up the elevator any second."

I had just read Myla's text saying she was walking into the lobby. I was shocked that Brayden and I had pulled this surprise off, but somehow, with the help of our friends and teammates, we had been able to do it.

I heard the ding of the elevator and the front door opening. I flicked on the lights as everyone yelled "Surprise!" when Myla walked in.

"What the hell?" she exclaimed, throwing one of her leather gloves at me and the other at her brother. "What did you two do? Is this why I wasn't allowed to go into the garage this morning, Bray?"

He wrapped his arms around his sister. "It's your twenty-first birthday; can't your brother and boyfriend surprise you?"

"Thank you." She hooked her arm around my

waist. "This is amazing, guys."

"Let the party begin!" I popped a bottle of Moet, pouring Myla a glass. "And for your first legal drink, some bubbly, my lady."

She sipped from her flute and her eyes got wide. "Holy shit! Is this what heaven tastes like?"

I kissed her forehead. "I think heaven tastes like s'mores with candied bacon on them, but we can chase it down with champagne for sure."

Ushering Myla around, Brayden and I made sure she was introduced to everyone at the party.

A cute girl walked in, looking around. "Excuse me," Brayden said before trotting over to her.

"Who's that?" I whispered to Myla.

The excitement on her face was contagious. "Karla. She was my nurse when I had my accident. She and Brayden have been dating on and off for a few months. I'm glad she came."

I glanced over to see Brayden go in for a quick kiss and I couldn't help but be excited for him.

Sean and Jessica were taking a smoke break out on the balcony when I took Myla by the hand and took her out to meet my best friend of all time.

"Sean, this has been long overdue."

He hugged Myla. "It's so nice to finally meet the person I have heard about nonstop for what feels like forever."

Jessica started laughing. "And then Sean keeps filling me in so I feel like I know you already."

Myla and Jessica started to hit it off. "Ok." Myla got her serious face on. "McBee, how the hell do you get your liquid eyeliner so fucking perfect? Half the time I stab myself in the eye with that shit and then it looks like I have been crying for a week with weird clown makeup on."

Jessica hooked her arm with Myla's. "How about I show you? I don't leave home without my makeup essentials."

Myla bounced a little before kissing me on the cheek. "Be back in a minute, we're going to take over your bathroom."

"It's not like your stuff hasn't already started to cover the counter, babe," I called back to her.

Sean nudged me. "Great party, man. Myla seems great."

I took in a long breath, looking through the sliding glass doors at my teammates and friends mingling and dancing, having a blast. Jordan was even doing a flaming bottle flare demo with a few of the bartenders she brought with her.

"Should I be worried that Jordan is going to light my place on fire?"

Sean tensed his shoulders, throwing his hands up. "I think you have maybe a twenty percent chance of that going horribly wrong, but that's what insurance is for, right?"

I gulped down the rest of my glass of Moet. "You're right. When you're right, you're right."

Sean cocked his head, furrowing his brow. "You all right? You seem nervous."

I pulled a black box out of my pocket and his jaw dropped. "I'm not going to ask her tonight, but I am going to ask Brayden's permission, and I figured showing him the rock would help him agree to it."

Myla

"So, you have to tell me—what's it like?" Jessica was fixing up my eyeliner while I sat on the bathroom counter.

"What's what like?" I asked, trying to hold as still as possible.

She pulled away to check out the first eye. "Sleeping with Gavin. I bet he's incredible."

I got instant goose bumps from even thinking about the morning sex we'd had to ring in my birthday. "It's complete and total ecstasy. I really don't know how else to describe it. The way he growls when I'm pleasing him—gah! It's just so amazing. I never thought I would be able to feel so much from one man, ya know?"

McBee's face lit up when she finished her masterpiece. "Hearing a guy moan because of you is the sexiest compliment ever."

"I really couldn't agree more."

Jessica narrowed her gaze. "Is it just me or did it get really quiet all of a sudden?"

I hopped off the counter, ready to go investigate. "Yeah, it did."

As it turned out, walking into an awkward silence was the least of my worries. Brayden came up next to me and said, "You might want to go see if Gavin is okay. Some chick walked in and he marched her right out into the hallway."

I rushed out the front door to see a woman crying and Gavin yelling at her. "After all these years you pick tonight of all fucking nights to come to my fucking home?"

"Gavin, please, I'm sorry!"

I stood in silence, trying to figure out what was going on.

"It's way too late for that. Just because my mother called you to tell you I've finally found true happiness with someone else gives you no fucking right."

The woman was on her knees, groveling at his feet. "But, I love you."

"Fuck you!"

Every cell in my body was buzzing. "Gavin?" I whimpered.

He turned to me with rage across his face. "Myla!" He let out a deep breath. "This is Marsheila and she was just leaving."

Her bleached hair was sticking to her damp face as she clambered to her feet. "I'm sorry for dropping in like this."

I grabbed Gavin's hand. "I think he said you were leaving." I stared her down before hitting the elevator button for her.

She shuffled away like a beat puppy with her tail between her legs. "I didn't mean to ruin your party."

I gave her a shit-eating grin. "Oh honey, you could never ruin my night. Thank you for leaving him so I could find the man of my dreams."

Once the door closed, Gavin pulled me up into his arms. "I am so sorry about that, baby. My mom doesn't know how to mind her own business."

I kissed him. "It's not your fault, but I think we have a room full of guests and a party to continue."

Gavin

As the party started to die down, Myla and I took seats at my wet bar while Jordan started to pack up her supplies.

"Good party, Hayes." Jordan handed Myla another

Jack and Coke.

"Thanks you," she said before turning to me. "Hey, babe." She slouched on the barstool, putting her bare feet up onto my lap. It was so adorable to me how drunk she was, her hair a mess, makeup smearing a little, eyes glassing over a bit. It wasn't the drunkenness that was the endearing part; it was seeing my girl in another light. Even fucked up out of her skull, she still gave me her little crooked grin and lit up a bit when she spoke to me.

"What's up, hotcakes?" I asked, trying to not laugh too much at her cuteness.

"You're the bestest boyfriend anyone could ask for in the history of ever." Myla's tiny hand landed with a thud on my thigh as she slurred before trying to take another sip of her Jack and Coke, completely missing the straw and chasing it around the glass for a bit.

"I think it's time to call it a night. What do you think?" I took the drink out of her hand and handed it back over to Jordan, who downed it in one gulp.

She pursed her lips and, serious as a heart attack, shook her head, yelling, "Dobby has no master! Dobby is a free elf!"

I couldn't help but laugh right there on the spot. "God, even drunk, you're still a nerd."

I scooped her up into my arms and carried her to bed. "I'll be right back. I'm just going to help Brayden and Jordan pack up the rest of the stuff and get it downstairs."

"Did the birthday girl go down without a fight?" Brayden was wiping down my kitchen counter as Jordan started packing up the last of the liquor bottles she had brought with her.

I shoved my hand down into my pocket, nervously fidgeting with the ring box that had been there all night.

"Brayden, can I have a minute?" I waved him toward the balcony.

"Yeah, sure. I'll be right back." He glanced over at Karla and she nodded while sitting on a barstool chatting with Jordan and Simon.

After shutting the door behind us, Brayden rubbed the back of his neck. "What's up?"

I took in a deep breath. "I love your sister."

He nodded. "Yeah man, tell me something I don't know."

I pulled the box out from my pocket. "She's perfect and I know you're going to say this is all really sudden. I'm not going to do it right away; I just wanted you to know where my head is at with all this, how serious I am about Myla."

"Dude, no one is perfect, and you're right, this is really sudden and fucking fast as shit." He started pacing around the balcony.

"You're right. No one is perfect." I sighed, shoving the box back into my pocket. "But, she's damn near it, and fucking perfect for me."

He leaned onto the railing. "I have to hand it to you, you really are falling for my sister. I hate and love it all at the same time."

"So, may I have your blessing?" Brayden nodded and I literally jumped in the hair, yelling, "Fuck yes!"

He pointed his finger at me, smiling wide. "Don't make me regret this, Hayes."

"I promise. I am going to spend the rest of my life making that girl as happy as humanly possible."

After making sure everyone had safe rides home and the apartment was at least somewhat clean, crawling into bed was the best feeling ever.

I pulled Myla into me, curling my body around her. In a sleepy daze she kissed the air, muttering, "Love you," before resting her head on my shoulder.

I had always been told that the best parts of life were the small, nameless moments spent smiling with someone you love, and in that bed with Myla sleeping soundly in my arms, I truly knew what that meant.

EPILOGUE

Myla

Months later

Rolling over, Gavin's bristly scruff rubbed against my cheek. His playoff beard was coming in strong and the only way I could describe how handsome Gavin looked was *downright panty-melting.*

I kissed his soft lips. "Baby, are you ready for tonight?" I whispered.

He wrapped his leg around mine, shushing me. "Not if I don't get my beauty rest, My."

I was wide awake, probably way more excited for game seven of the playoffs than he was. Gavin peeked at me with only one eye open, then whistled for Seven, who jumped onto the bed panting and wagging her tail, jingling more than normal.

I noticed that she had a ribbon tied around her neck. Gavin reached up and pulled out the bow, letting three rings drop onto my bare stomach.

He leaned up on one elbow as tears started to

flood my eyes.

"Myla, I have thought about how to ask this for months now, but I knew the simplest, intimate moments for us were both of our favorites." He took the ring that had a solitaire canary diamond and slid it onto my finger. "Please, spend the rest of your life with me."

I stared at the shimmering stone, completely in shock.

"Say something." He sighed.

I gasped for breath. "Of course! Yes!" Grabbing the other two rings, I looked over to Gavin, who had the biggest grin on his hairy face. "What are these for?"

"Well, you know how nontraditional we both think these things should be. So, I might have taken care of all of the arrangements." He tossed me his shirt from the floor and pulled on a pair of gym shorts. "You might want to put that on for this next part."

Yanking the huge shirt over my head, Gavin opened our bedroom door. On the other side was my brother dressed in a tux, standing next to Karla—whose baby bump was finally starting to pop out—in a gorgeous floor-length dress. Brayden was holding a white dress bag and walking into the room.

"Are we getting married today?" I started hysterically crying.

"Everyone is waiting at our house, including Sean, who got ordained to marry you online last week. We have a hairdresser and makeup artist waiting in the living room for you."

Karla started giggling. "Did you really think I wanted to try on all those different dresses to get your opinion *just* in case Brayden decided to make an honest woman out of me?"

She shoved my brother as he started laughing. "What we have going on is working, why complicate it with marriage? No offense, Gavin."

Gavin pulled his tux out of the closet and started polishing his dress shoes. "None taken." He looked over at me. I was still in shock. "Chop, chop, little girl. We're all waiting on you now."

Karla grabbed the dress from Brayden. "Why don't you two head over to the house and help finish getting set up? We have a wedding to get to and a game to win."

As I was sitting on a barstool, getting my hair curled and airbrush makeup applied, Karla unzipped the dress bag. "So, this is the one I made you try on a few weeks ago. I remembered it was your favorite."

She pulled out a gorgeous off-white, lace mermaid-style dress with a sweetheart neckline. Within less than an hour I was in my dress, riding in the back of a limo with Karla, on the way to my childhood home.

"I hope they're all set up and ready to go." I was getting nervous that there wasn't going to be enough time for the wedding and to get the guys to the rink in time.

Karla put a reassuring hand on mine, pouring me a glass of champagne. "We have it all timed perfectly, love. This is going to be great and we're going to the game tonight."

"I thought Brayden said we weren't allowed to be there."

The car pulled over and Karla paused before opening the door. "Gavin was pretty convincing. They started the season with a win, seems fitting that they end the playoffs with you there too. You're his luck, My. Don't ever forget that."

Standing at the altar, staring into Gavin's stormy eyes with all our closest family and friends standing in a circle around us, it finally hit me—I was about to become Mrs. Myla Hayes.

"And do you, Gavin, take Myla to be your wife?" Sean was way too adorable in his dress uniform, helping us tie the knot.

"I do." Gavin leaned down and kissed my cheek.

"Hey, no kissing the bride until I say so."

Gavin chuckled. "Hey, playing by the rules is never as fun."

After rolling his eyes at Gavin's remark, Sean looked to me. "And do you, Myla, take this goofball to be your husband?"

I yelled at the top of my lungs, "Heck yes, I do!"

Everyone started popping bottles of champagne

and toasting.

"You may *now* kiss your lovely bride." The crowd erupted as Gavin scooped me up into his arms.

"Now, you're my girl, forever. How does that sound Mrs. Hayes?"

Hearing those words roll off his lips sent electricity throughout my entire body.

"Absolutely perfect."

Brayden slapped Gavin on the shoulder, addressing the whole group of people. "We have a game to get to, ladies and gents. Feel free to hang out. I set up TVs throughout the house so everyone can watch. Game seven here we come!"

Seven trotted over to Brayden, wagging her tail. "Not you, girl." He threw the tennis ball she had dropped at his feet.

"All right, my love. There's only one more surprise, but it's at the rink. Simon and Karla will walk you through it. See you soon." Gavin kissed me goodbye and ran out the front door with Brayden and a few of their teammates that had come to wish us well.

After a few glasses of champagne, it was time to head to the arena. "Ok, I'll go change and then we can head out."

Karla grabbed my hand. "Nope. You're staying in that dress for a little while longer."

Simon threw the strap of a duffle bag over his

shoulder. "I have a change of clothes for each of us in here for when the time comes."

Walking through the crowd of fans in a wedding dress was hilarious. Everyone kept stopping to stare as Karla and Simon escorted me to the very same seat I had occupied for that first game, right next to the penalty box.

We were only in our seats for a few minutes before the announcer came over the loudspeaker. "Will Myla Hayes please make her way to the Otters' locker room? Again, Myla Hayes, please make your way to the Otters' locker room."

Gavin was waiting for me by the locked stairway to escort me down to the locker room. He was already in his pads and jersey.

"What's going on?" I asked as he grabbed my hand.

"You'll see." We rushed down to where the team was hooting and hollering for us. "Congrats, guys!"

Gavin's father threw an arm around me. "Welcome to the family, kid." It had taken him and his wife a while to get used to the idea of me, but they had finally come around.

I wrapped my arms around his neck. "Thank you!"

The opposing team was being announced and flooding onto the ice.

"Ready babe?" Gavin threw me up into his arms.

"Ready for what?"

The announcer started to get the fans fired up.

"And the Otters have a very special announcement they would like to share with all of you this evening. Let's give a huge welcome to your team, the Otters!" The fans exploded, leaping onto their feet.

Crosby led the way and Gavin followed him with me still swept up into his arms. "You might want to hold on tight, baby."

He skated out onto the ice, my flowing dress trailing behind him as we made our way to center ice.

"Congratulations to the captain, Gavin Hayes, who tied the knot to this beauty only a few hours ago."

The entire team started skating around us, waving their sticks in the air, cheering.

The moment had to be fleeting as Gavin skated me back over so I could head back up to my seat. "I love you!" he yelled, skating backward away from me.

I met Simon at the top of the stairs and he handed me my favorite jeans and a jersey that had Gavin's number on it.

He whispered into my ear, "Check out the back. This is my favorite!"

Turning the jersey over, I saw the name on it read *Mrs. Hayes*.

The events of the day started to really sink in and I started crying as I pulled the jersey over my wedding dress.

"Let's go watch my man kill it out there!"

The game was incredible—fast paced, high scoring, lots of fights. Once the Otters were up by three points in the last two minutes, Gavin picked a fight just to prove a point. After they brawled all the way to the ice, the refs broke them up.

Gavin sitting in the penalty box next to me was infuriating and awesome all at once. He yelled over to me, "Hey wifey!"

I got right up against the glass. "Yes husband?" I hollered back to him.

"Kiss me!"

We pressed our lips against the cold glass separating us.

Best fucking wedding day kiss ever.

The end.

All books by
Kristen Hope Mazzola

The Crashing Series:
Crashing: The Wedding: Cali's Story (Crashing #0.5)
Crashing Back Down (Crashing #1)
Falling Back Together (Crashing #2)

The Unacceptables MC Standalone Series:
Unacceptable
Unspeakable

The Hysterics Standalone Series:
The Hysterics
Colt & Serena: A Hysterics Short Story

Standalones:
Stupid Hearts
Rough & Tumble
Hat Trick

SNEAK PEAK:
UNACCEPTABLE

AN UNNACEPTABLES MC ROMANCE
KRISTEN HOPE MAZZOLA

CHAPTER 1.

Slam!

The sound of my mom throwing her hair dryer across their room and it crashing through the thin walls of our doublewide jolted me from my deep sleep.

"Why don't you just leave then, you fucking scumbag?" She was messed up again, slurring her words together as she picked another fight with my father after coming home in the early hours of the morning.

"Don't you freaking tempt me Helen, I swear to fucking God." My dad's raspy voice was low and gravely, probably trying to not wake me.

Too late.

This fight wasn't like every other night that she came home late from the bar; this one sounded worse.

"If you want to leave so badly, then just do me a damn favor and get the hell out, you rat bastard." I heard their door open and the sound of my dad's boots stomping down the hallway with the light thudding of my mom trying to run after him in heels.

"Helen, get the hell off me. Enough is enough." He was right outside my door. I held my breath. I was ready to run away with him.

"You damn asshole you're not taking her with you!"

Slap!

Slap!

Slap!

I could hear her hitting him.

"You're not going to raise my daughter, you fucking, no good, whore. I'll leave her here over my dead body!" That was the first night I ever heard that word: whore. It was the perfect definition for my mother. It was exactly what she was.

I heard my mother's sobs getting softer as my dad slowly opened the door to my room. I held my breath, trying to pretend I was still asleep, silently begging him to pick me up in his strong arms and whisk me away from the trailer park and the terrible person that pretended to be a good mother.

"Yes. Hello." I heard her meek voice crack as she sniffled into the receiver of our old yellow corded phone in the kitchen. "My boyfriend is trying to kidnap my daughter. Please send someone fast."

"You damn—you goddamned cunt! She's my daughter too."

"Fuck you, Rave! If you wanted her to be your daughter so badly, you should have signed the damn birth certificate!"

The front door swung open and my father's boots trudged down the metal steps, the sound echoing in my ears as my heart got heavier with each stomp. I ran to the window and watched my hero, my savior, the only person that ever showed me love get in his truck and drive away.

Taillights. That's really what I remembered from that night. The glow of the taillights of my father's rusty, clunking white long-bed. The gravel spit out from under the tires as he ran away to his freedom. Who could blame him? Not me, that's for damn sure. I was about to follow in his footsteps. It had only taken me seventeen years to grow the metaphorical balls to realize that he was right. He had made the right move. All of the resentment and anger I had displaced onto him for abandoning me was finally falling on the right shoulders: hers, my fucking whore of a mother.

I sat outside the trailer I'd grown up in, in the same spot my dad had escaped from, watching the light switch off in my mom's room from the front seat of my beat up Camaro. She was probably overdramatically faking another orgasm while john-number-five-hundred-and-something believed every grunt and groan. I had to hand it to her: she was damn good at her job.

I took the worn pages of the letter I had read thousands of times and stuffed them back into the envelope. I read the city name in the return address again: *Vilas.* That's where I'd start my new life. That's where I'd start my search, not for him, but for myself. If it was good enough for my father, it'd be good enough for me.

It had been ten years since I'd gotten my only letter from him. It was my most cherished possession. I knew the whole thing by heart, but the last line stuck with me, like a broken record in my mind:

I have always loved you and I always will, never forget that, Princess.

Getting that handwritten note changed my life. It gave me hope, courage, and a fire under my butt to make something better of myself. In the back of my head I knew that it was only one short letter, that if he truly loved me like he had so dramatically claimed, he would have come back for me, fought for me, even stayed that night, but that was all in the past. It was time to start the future and for fuck's sake, I was about to take the bull by the horns and be something more than a trailer park critter that stripped to make ends meet.

The old engine cried to life after the third time I turned the key. I really needed to get it looked at, but I needed to get the hell out of the trailer park first. I had no plan, just a stack of uncashed paychecks from the Pink Kitty, where I had been working for years, and a wad of dollar bills that I had managed to hide from my mother, but it would have to be enough. I had hit the wall and was finally able to see it: I needed to move on.

I did have to give her some credit where it was due: my mom tried. She loved me in her own way, but she was never loving or motherly. She was either high or fucking to get her next fix for most of my childhood, but that was ok; I was over it. I'd realized long ago that you can't ask more of someone than they are capable of; she was nothing more than a hooker, and I had to accept it. My mom had no aspiration to make something more of herself and I would have to live with that. There is no saving someone that doesn't want to be saved, that's for damn sure.

I glanced back in my rearview mirror as the dusty road took me away from the only home I had ever known.

Hopefully this will be my last look at that hellhole.

I jammed out to Katy Perry and T-Swift while shifting and grinding gears as the road twisted and turned, my long black curls dancing in the wind coming in through the open windows. Liberation boiled in my veins while a sting of guilt bit at the back of my mind. I knew that she would figure out later rather than sooner that I had ditched her. It probably wouldn't be until she went to raid my room for my stash of money that I tried to hide from working all those damn late nights for nasty truckers and slime balls.

I drove and drove, stopping for gas a handful of times, having to fill up the clutch and power steering fluid on a few occasions, and ignoring my body's aching need for a bed. I desperately wanted to put as much road and as many states as humanly possible between me and the shithole I was crawling out of. Coffee and chocolate donut holes would have to do until I just couldn't take it any longer.

The day droned on and my eyelids got heavier and heavier as a slow Boyz II Men song poured from the speakers. That's when I finally saw it, the sign that I had been waiting for: "Vilas – 5 miles".

177

Heck yes!

I was as giddy as a schoolgirl as joy consumed me. I felt like I had finally made it. This wasn't just a dream built up in the mind of a naive child. It was real. I was finally free. I could fucking taste the sweet victory as I breathed in the dusty road that was leading the way to my salvation.

As I pulled off the highway and turned down a back country road, the exhaustion started to settle in deep. A yawn took over as I made my way into a dive-looking bar's parking lot. I needed to find a place to crash and figure out my next move. I grabbed the bright red lipstick from my bag; even though I felt and probably looked like shit, lipstick would make it a little better. Two things I never left the house without: a good bra and lipstick.

A handwritten "Help Wanted" sign caught my eye as I pulled on the worn metal handle. The smell of cigarette smoke wafted out as I swung the heavy wooden door open. It felt like an old movie where the music cuts out when the main character mistakenly walks into a bar that outsiders aren't welcome in. There were a few empty bar tables scattered around and a handful of pool tables in the back.

I took a seat at one of the creaking swivel barstools at least five seats away from the next patron. Every eye was glued on me as I threw my purse down on the bar with a thud and waved to the older bartender. It made me a little bit more uneasy when I realized I was the only person with a vagina in the whole joint. A few of the guys at the pool table behind me nearly broke their necks as I walked in with my tight skinny jeans, pushup bra, and flowy yoga top.

The bartender meandered over my way while I got a good look into his kind honey eyes; his shaved bald, shiny head; and the pure white, long handlebar mustache that rested over his curling lips. His rosy cheeks made him look far more jolly than he probably was. What really caught my eye was the cut that he was wearing. I'd definitely wandered into the wrong bar where outsiders were not welcome in the slightest.

I look a deep breath and reminded myself that I was a tall skinny chick and that my gun was only a foot away in my handbag. After working as a stripper for the better part of five years, I'd learned quickly that I needed to know how to protect myself and to not let fear ever cross my face.

In a slow drawl, his voice cracked the silence, "Can I get you somethin', sweetheart?"

I swallowed hard before answering, "A bottle of Bud Light, please." I felt like a mouse would have spoken louder than I just had, but he nodded and reached into the ice trough in front of him to grab my beer.

"Do I know you from somewhere?" His pale honey eyes narrowed; he was studying my face pretty intently. I glanced over to my bag where the only letter that I had from my father was concealed next to my three-eighty bodyguard. He very well could be in this bar or know this bartender. The town was small enough.

I shook my head. "I've never been here before."

"I think I would remember meeting you." He winked with a throaty chuckle before looking over to help a man in a matching cut that just had sat down next to me.

The newcomer ordered his whiskey on the rocks and leisurely turned in my direction. I glanced at the back of the bartender just long enough to read the club's name scrolled across the back: The Unacceptables. Glancing over, my cheeks flared red as I took in the features of the young biker to my right. Everything faded into a blurry background when the extremely tall, broad-chested stud smiled at me. His lips were the perfect shade of light red, pierced with two small hoops in the left corner, and even his eyes smiled as his gaze met mine.

"Hello there." He slid his stool closer to mine.

I shook my head quickly, trying to get my wits about me while his deep blues were threatening to drown me. "Hi." I sipped from my beer slowly, fighting to hide how nervous I had become all of a sudden.

"Not from around here are you?" The bartender slid his drink in front of him.

"Nope. Just passing through."

I read the words "vice president" on the front of his cut before I let my mind start to focus completely on how breathtakingly handsome this man truly was.

Slow. Deep. Breaths.
Slow.
Deep.
Don't let him catch you practically drooling.
Damn, he's gorgeous.

"That's a shame." His lip curled under his piercings as his tongue rolled over the silver hoops gently. "I'm Abel." He held out his hand for me to take.

"Nice to meet you, I'm Crickett."

"Wait." He tried desperately not to laugh as his cheeks got red and his lips pulled up at the corners. "Your name is Crickett? Like chirp chirp?"

"Yep, it sure is." I rolled my eyes before taking a long swig from the bottle. "I'm named after a damn insect."

"Who would ever think to name their kid that?" He was full blown laughing now as the hilarity of my unfortunate name really sunk in deep.

"A deadbeat and a hooker."

The bartender practically jogged down the bar after my name hit the air and gave Abel a stern look. "Table. Now!"

"Everything all right, Bucky?"

The gruff old man narrowed his eyes. "The meeting was supposed to start fifteen minutes ago, son. I'll be up in a second. Rich is looking for ya."

Another bartender without a cut on slid behind the bar and all of the bikers filed through a door at the back of the bar. Abel was gone in a flash, without the slightest goodbye.

The young guy—who couldn't be much older than eighteen judging by his patchy beard mixed with peach fuzz—walked over to me. "Miss? Care for another?" He pointed at my almost empty bottle and I nodded.

After taking a sip of the fresh icy cold amber goodness, I looked up at the guy playing on his phone. "Do you know a good motel close by?"

He smiled, glancing up from the screen. "Oh yeah, we have one just a block north of here, right off the main road. Can't miss it."

"Great, thanks. What's your name?" I felt chatty, even bored, and I was great at flirty small talk. I figured, why not chat up this cutie and hopefully get some details about Abel?

"Me? I'm Holt."

"Oh crap, I almost forgot." I dug the koozie out of my purse and placed it on my beer.

Holt's eyebrow raised.

"What? You don't want cold hands or warm beer."

"Yeah. I guess you're right."

"Are you from around here, Holt?" I twirled a long curl between my fingers and stared into his dark brown eyes.

"Born and raised." His drawl was thick as he wiped the bar top with a wet towel. "What about you?"

"I'm from a few states over. Making a break for it." I chugged half my beer.

"Running ain't always a bad thing. Vilas is a good town. Hopefully you'll like it here."

"How much do I owe you for these?"

I bit my lip slowly and watched Holt's cheeks flare as he rubbed the back of his neck and stuttered a bit. "It was taken care of." He held up his hand to stop me from taking my wallet out of my purse.

I raised my eyebrow at him. "Really?"

He nodded. "Abel told me to put it on his tab. So you're good to go."

Wow. Sweet, mysterious, and hot. I might have to give this town and Abel a trial run.

"Thanks, Holt. Maybe I'll see you around."

He nodded. "Hope you get some rest."

"I look that bad, huh?"

Holt smiled sweetly as he shook his head. "Nah, you just look like you've been traveling for a while and need a hot shower and a bed."

"Well then I look the way I feel. That Abel guy, he's all right?" I should have been more subtle, but I was worn out and beating around the bush seemed more draining than what it was worth.

"Yeah, he's one of the best guys I know. Tough skin but a fucking heart of gold."

"Good to know." I chugged the rest of my beer and threw a couple dollars on the bar. Holt's sweet smile spread wider as the guys came back out from the backroom, or abyss, or wherever they'd all run off to in such a hurry. To my dismay, Abel was not in the group that filed back into their bar seats. I waved goodbye to Holt and made my way to finally get the shuteye that I desperately needed.

CHAPTER 2.

Rounding the corner, I saw the neon vacancy light shining bright above the motel's front office door. The dimly lit gravel parking lot crunched under the tires of my crying car. It was time to put more power steering fluid in for sure. I grabbed the plastic bottle of fluid from the floorboard of the passenger side and fixed the problem. At least there were a few things I could do under the hood of my car to make it run at a somewhat decent level. Growing up where most of the guys around built mud trucks had its perks from time to time.

Looking around as I made my way into the office, I noticed a few cars scattered around the lot, all with out of state plates. It was nice to know that other out-of-towners stopped there. It shouldn't have made a difference, but it comforted me to know that other travelers felt safe enough to crash there too.

The bell chimed above my head as I walked into the small office that smelled like mothballs and stale pizza. A sweet girl peeked up from a school book the was laid out on the counter. "Hey miss. Lookin' for a room?"

I nodded. "Sure am."

"Smoking or nonsmoking?"

Even though I was a smoker, the thought of stale cigarette smoke embedded in the pillows made me want to hurl on the spot.

"Nonsmoking."

"All right. I just need a credit card to hold the room. How many nights will you be our guest?"

For not being more than thirteen, she was very articulate and polite. I was pretty impressed by her.

"I'm not sure, actually." I dug my hands into my pockets; it felt unnerving as hell to not have any plan whatsoever.

"Longer than a week?"

I shrugged. "Possibly."

"We have weekly specials, you'll save fifty bucks that way."

"Sounds like a plan to me."

"Perfect." She punched a few keys on the dinosaur of a computer that was in front of me. "If anything changes, just come on in and let us know." Her kind eyes and sweet smile settled down my growing nerves as she handed me a key with a giant red plastic ornament-looking keychain on it.

"You're on the first floor, three doors over on the left."

I handed her my credit card and license. "All right, Miss Hayes. You're all set."

"Thanks." With a quick wave, I was off to finally lie down in a bed for a much needed night's sleep, even though it was still the afternoon.

The light shining through the window stung my tired eyes as I groggily started to wake up. I had no idea what time I had actually crashed the day before. I'd barely even had time to turn the lights off before I hit the pillow and passed out, let alone undress, take off my makeup, or look at the clock.

Rolling over, bright red numbers blared eleven fifteen at me as my stomach started to rumble. After peeling myself from the pillow-topped mattress that felt like a lumpy heaven, I dug through the duffle bag that contained my life until I found my favorite pair of jeans and a yoga top.

I glanced at the bright red smear on the pillow from my favorite lipstick and the black dots from my mascara. Thankfully I was not the one that was going to have to wrestle with those stains.

Within minutes the faucet was pumping steaming water into the tub. A nice long soak felt like a dream for my tired body. The trip hadn't been emotional until it all crashed onto me as I sunk to the bottom of that porcelain bath. I was free. I was finally freaking free, and I felt bad about it.

The image of my mom figuring out that I was gone broke into my mind and ripped my heart apart. But who was I kidding? If she hadn't started blowing up my phone yet, she had no idea. She was probably still in a haze of meth and booze from another week-long binge.

Right before I left, I could tell that's where she was heading anyway. It was the perfect time to escape: I would be so far gone by the time she was halfway conscious that it wouldn't matter.

"Critter!" Her hollow cry came from the back bedroom.

I rolled my eyes at her dumbass nickname for me. Wasn't my real name bad enough?

"Yeah Ma?"

"Get me a fucking coke from the fridge."

I grabbed the last can of soda from the barren wasteland she called a refrigerator.

I hurriedly popped the top and walked it back to her where she was laying in bed, sick as a dog from yet another withdrawal.

"Here. I gotta get to work."

Her shaking hand wrapped around the can as her sunken, dark eyes begged me for mercy. She didn't have to ask; I knew what I needed to do.

"Yeah. I think Vinnie is working tonight. I'll see what I can get."

"That's my girl. Thank you, Crit."

"I'll be back late though. Try to sleep and don't let anyone come over with you sick like this. I don't want this place to get robbed again."

I snapped out of my daze of strolling down terrible memory lane when the sound of splattering water echoed in the tiny bathroom. Looking over the side of the tub, I realized about half an inch of water was starting to coat the off white tiles.

Shit.

I lunged for the faucet, turned off the water, and sunk back in to relax and let my fingers and toes get pruney. I couldn't remember the last time I'd had time to relax like that. The quiet and the peacefulness were almost disturbing. It was a far cry from the cursing, fighting neighbors and my mom hollering at me or moaning in some john's ear all the time.

Good riddance to all that bull crap.

Giving in to my roaring stomach, I drained the water and got dressed. I laid towels on the floor of my soaking wet bathroom to lap up the water that had spilled over.

I made my way to the closest Waffle House my phone's GPS could find. Luckily it was just up the road and I had a hankering for greasy cooking and a pot of coffee. I quickly scarfed down some scattered, smothered, covered, and chunked hashbrowns with two eggs over easy on the side and tried to think about what my next move was going to be.

Not having a plan was both liberating and frustrating. I knew that the money I had was going to go faster than I could admit to myself. I checked the classified section for jobs while I sipped on hours-old coffee. I wasn't really built to be a stable hand, and I didn't think there was a strip joint in Vilas.

As I was getting up to pay my check, Holt and the older bartender walked through the front door. Holt ambled over to me with a sweet smile on his face.

"Nice to see you haven't left our little town yet. Thinkin' about sticking around?" He spit into a Dixie cup and I could smell the wintergreen chew that was wadded up in his lower lip.

I held up the paper and shrugged. "A girl's gotta eat and there ain't any jobs here for me it seems."

"Hey Bucky, aren't we still looking for a daytime bartender?"

He nodded. "Yeah, the one Abel hired last week quit on me Monday night."

"Well there ya have it. I'll talk to Abel about it. Come by in a few hours and we'll get ya all set up."

Just like that I had a freaking job in a town I wasn't even sure I was going to stay in. At least I knew I was going to be able to keep a roof over my head and hopefully finance another move, if nothing else.

DID YOU ENJOY WHAT YOU JUST READ?

RATE IT: If the answer is yes, you did enjoy Hat Trick, please consider putting up a review on **Amazon** and/or **Goodreads**

SHARE IT: Please help spread the word about Hat Trick. Tell your friends and family about it or share it with them. Sharing is caring, after all.

STAY CONNECTED: Follow Kristen Hope Mazzola on **facebook.com/authorkristenhope** or **twitter.com/khmazz** to stay up to date about new releases, giveaways, and so much more! Also, join Kristen's email mailing list for her monthly newsletter: **www.kristenhopemazzola.com/mailing-list.html**

SPECIAL THANKS

TO DAYNA: There is no way to thank you enough. You are my right hand, my calm, my ride or die. I would never have had confidence in myself without you. In every way, you are the best!

TO JORDAN: Oh men, girl! You are freaking amazing. Thanks for letting me friend zone you, for all of the texts of encouragement, for letting me tease the ever-loving-crap out of you.

TO MARY CATHERINE: I don't know what I would do without our talks. You have become one of my best friends. Thank goodness for Vegas!

TO HEATHER: I am so thankful we got to meet at Submit and Devour 2016 in Miami. You have turned into such an important person in my life. You will forever by my author whisperer!

TO TRIBE: You ladies have been so instrumental in keeping me going, even when I was ready to throw in the towel. You guys have been there cheering me on at every turn and y'all are just so awesome.

TO KAYLA: Hahaha...oh you! You're my sister in every way possible and I flove you! Thanks for letting me put you into one of my favorite scenes in this book, face-fucking and all!

TO C. MARIE: You're the freaking best and without your editing genius, I would be lost. You put up with so much of my crap and turn my mangled babbles into beautiful words!

TO MCBEE: I am so excited for your character! You have turned into one badass chick and I cannot wait to see what is in store for her in the feature!

TO MARSHEILA: Thanks for letting me turn you into an awesome jerk of a character and for leaving Gavin at the altar. You are amazing and I love all of our antics at signings!

TO J-FLO: You're my homie and I love you! (even though you jokingly told me to do this, I still mean it.)

TO RICH: Thanks for talking out these sex scenes with me and inspiring some steamy shit. It's been interesting and fun, to say the least.

TO DAWN/DANIELLE: You are incredible! Thanks for writing the Hers Series and letting me take a section of Ryder to put into this book. I cannot wait to see what the book world has in store for us in the future!

TO PATTI: You are freaking great! I am so glad that we're working together now and I am so thankful for your friendship.

NOTE FROM THE AUTHOR

Thank you for buying my novel. In doing so, you have helped fulfill a very important goal of mine. From every purchase of any of my books, I donate to the Marcie Mazzola Foundation. The mission of the foundation is to "help better the lives of abused and at-risk children; and to build community awareness regarding the needs of children."

The Marcie Mazzola Foundation was established in 2003 by my family. On July 6, 2002, Marcie died tragically in an automobile accident. Although she was only 21 at the time of her death, Marcie had experienced many things and touched many lives. She was a beautiful young woman whose inner beauty surpassed even her physical beauty because of her compassionate nature and treatment of others.

At the time of her death, Marcie was involved in a civil lawsuit against a school bus driver who had sexually abused her when she was 11 years old. Prior to her death, it had been expected that the case would be won, but since Marcie could no longer testify, it was going to be next to impossible to win. Marcie's attorney met with her family to determine if the suit should be continued. He advised the family that Marcie had confided in him her intention to donate her entire award to help sexually and physically abused children if she won the case. Once this was known, the family had no doubt that the suit had to continue.

The attorney's strong commitment to Marcie prompted him to proceed with the case, and against all odds, it was won.

Marcie's estate was awarded a monetary settlement. With her attorney's guidance and continued support, the family established a foundation as a tribute to Marcie's life, which would continue her legacy to help children.

To learn more about The Marcie Mazzola Foundation, please visit: http://www.marciemazzolafoundation.org

Marcie Mazzola Foundation
158 Burr Road, Commack, NY 11725
phone: 631-858-1855 • fax: 631-462-8544
email: info@marciemazzolafoundation.org

THE AUTHOR

Hi! I am just an average twenty-something following my dreams. I have a full time "day job" and by night I am an author. I guess you could say that writing is like my super power (I always wanted one of those). I am a lover of wine, sushi, football and the ocean; that is when I am not wrapped up in the literary world.

Please feel free to contact me to chat about my writing, books you think I'd like or just to shoot the, well you know.

Stay Connected:

KristenHopeMazzola.com

https://www.facebook.com/AuthorKristenHope

https://twitter.com/khmazz

Email: authorkristenmazzola@gmail.com

62309301R00119

Made in the USA
Charleston, SC
12 October 2016